J

)9

MacPherson's
Lament

SV

MacPherson's Lament

An Elizabeth MacPherson Mystery

◆

Sharyn McCrumb

M
MCC
1992

BALLANTINE BOOKS
NEW YORK

Copyright © 1992 by Sharyn McCrumb

ISBN 0-345-36576-3

Manufactured in the United States of America

For Joe Blades of Missouri,
now working behind Union lines

◆

ACKNOWLEDGMENTS

THERE ARE A NUMBER of distinguished and talented members of the legal profession who are no doubt hoping that I will not drag their names into these proceedings, but since no good deed goes unpunished, I would like to thank the following attorneys for conspiring in the plotting of this novel. Any legal errors herein are the result of the author's ignoring the advice of counsel. Special thanks to Ohio Judge Judith A. Cross, who egged me on in the very beginning, offering inspired—one might almost say "fiendish"—suggestions on how to get a young attorney into serious trouble.

Additional legal advice was generously provided by attorneys Julian Cannell; H. Gregory Campbell, Jr.; David Hood; Erik Hildinger; and by Virginia State Senator Madison Marye.

MacPherson's
Lament

Why were they all going out to war?

He brooded a moment. It wasn't slavery.
That stale red-herring of Yankee knavery.
Nor even states-rights, at least not solely,
But something so dim that it must be holy.

—STEPHEN VINCENT BENÉT,
John Brown's Body, Book 2

PROLOGUE

RICHMOND—APRIL 2, 1865

GABRIEL HAWKS RECKONED that his extra pair of socks might dry before sunset on the warm deck of the *Virginia*, since the day was fine. It had been as good a day as a body could ask for in early spring—the sky like Jamaica water, with just enough wind to tickle the canvas and to bring a smell of flowers and new-plowed ground from the adjoining land. Captain Dunnington had tried to spoil the afternoon by ordering them all ashore to drill and march on the riverbank, but even that was tolerable on as fair a day as this. Better than staying crammed on the ironclad within quarters too narrow to swing a cat in—and nothing to do but think about being hungry on half rations. *And* listen to the rumble of distant cannons.

Gabe had never figured on being in any navy. In the sixteen years of his life before the war, he'd lived in the shadow of Bear Mountain in Giles County, Virginia, and he'd hardly even seen enough water to float a ship in. When the fighting commenced, he'd joined up with four other fellows from home.

He grew up on a small mountain farm, mostly apple orchards and a few head of cattle in steep pastureland. The Hawks were hard-pressed to feed even the younguns on what they produced, so they never owned slaves. Never needed any on a small place, and didn't much approve of that sort of soft life anyhow.

Gabe hadn't made up his mind about which side he favored in the war when Fort Sumter was fired on. By a margin of two to one the Virginia legislature had voted not to secede, and that was all right with him. But things were different two weeks later when Lincoln called on the states for militia to put down the insurrection: seventy-five thousand men were ordered to invade South Carolina and the other seceding states. Gabe couldn't hold with that—sending invaders onto a sister state's land. His mother's people had come from Carolina, down Salem way. So when Virginia joined the Confederacy, so did Gabriel Hawks.

Of course he hadn't figured on getting to be an officer. The South had seven military academies full of rich men's sons, and they were the ones commissioned. Gabe, a small and wiry mountain boy with Bible learning and no family influence to draw on, had been mustered into the infantry at the lowest rank. (And furnish your own clothes and weapons.) Still, he had been proud to be a private in the Stonewall Brigade. The Shenandoah Valley boys had cut such a swath through the Federals' ranks that they reckoned they could have fought the angels themselves to a standstill. But when General Jackson took a bullet two years back at Chancellorsville, he took the charm with him to the hereafter. Two of the boys from home had died after that, and Gabe had ended up in hospital with a burning fever that left him wasted and looking like a scarecrow. After he was well enough to be released, he'd been given new orders: a transfer to the navy.

At first he had been right glad of the change. If he couldn't be a hero in Jeb Stuart's cavalry, then he'd see what life was like at sea. No more marching in worn-out shoes, leaving your blood behind on the snow of the railroad tracks, and damned little chance to get shot, either. Maybe on a ship there'd be something besides hardtack to eat. Maybe they'd just sail right away from the whole war. He'd heard Confederate ships had been to Europe, the Caribbean—even the Pacific Ocean.

But he hadn't got far. Here he was at the mouth of the James River, within spitting distance of Richmond. The *Virginia* was an ironclad, the flagship of a fleet of eight, charged with the duty of guarding the capital from invasion by water. The three ironclads were moored across the only available channel in the James, their might bolstered by five wooden gunships and the naval batteries ashore. The crews remained there—cramped, hungry, and landlocked, waiting for it all to end.

Tom Bridgeford, who was standing at the rails looking out over the river, called out, "Come and wave, boys! Flag-of-truce boat coming by!"

Gabriel Hawks looked over the side as the little boat churned its way upriver. It was overflowing with newly released prisoners of war being repatriated to the Confederacy in a prisoner exchange with the Union. The freed soldiers laughed and whooped and let out a mighty yell when they saw the Confederate flag on the *Virginia*'s mast. Gabe waved to the cheering throng, but he did not smile.

"Damn fools," he said to Bridgeford. "What do they think we're going to feed them?"

"I don't reckon they know how bad it is," said Bridgeford as he watched them go.

"Then what do they reckon that booming is? A thunderstorm?"

The low rumble of cannon fire had been echoing across the water all afternoon. He'd heard talk of a battle in Petersburg, but that was nothing new. The fighting had been within earshot of Richmond for weeks now, but still the lines held, and spring came and church bells tolled, just like nothing was amiss.

Gabe Hawks grinned at lanky, redheaded Tom Bridgeford. "Why, I figured that rumbling was just my stomach complaining that my throat's been cut. It's been so long since I've sent any food down there."

"Too bad you're not back on your piss-ant farm," said Bridgeford. "You could just go out in the woods and shoot you something."

"I would, too," said Gabe. Bridgeford was a carpet knight from Wilmington who thought that potatoes grew on trees. "I reckon I could shoot me a wild pig that could feed—"

But Bridgeford wasn't listening. "Look what's coming!" he said. "Steamer, pulling alongside." A uniformed man stood waiting to board the ironclad. He looked grim and he held a package tightly under his arm as he stared up at the flag.

"What do you reckon he wants?" asked Gabe. He was only a master's mate, and the rituals of the flagship were strange to him.

Bridgeford sneered at such a tomfool question. "Admiral Semmes is aboard, isn't he? They just were sending dinner along to his cabin as I came up. It's probably some military intelligence for him."

"Maybe we're going to attack!" Gabe was tired of sitting in the river, listening to the war in echoes.

"In that case, let's play a hand of cards," said Bridgeford, reaching in his pocket for the worn and crumpled deck that had almost outlasted the war. "Might as well enjoy what's left of a perfect day."

"Play cards on Sunday?" cried Gabe.

Bridgeford shook his head. "Hawks, they're killing people in Petersburg. Do you think the Lord will notice a friendly hand of poker?"

They were still at it when twilight came and the order was given to get the ships under way for Drewry's Bluff.

"What are we going to do up there?" Gabe asked as a seaman hurried past.

The sailor stopped, wide-eyed, and whispered, "I overheard the admiral talking to his messenger. He says he's going to destroy the fleet!"

"Just before the battle, Mother"
—GEORGE FREDERICK ROOT,
Civil War song

CHAPTER

I

Edinburgh
June 8, 1992

Dear Bill,

There is a silly rumor going around the family that you have graduated from law school, passed the bar exam, and are actually setting yourself up in practice as a partner. I suppose that this will settle the betting pool once and for all. I wonder which one of us picked this decade as the probable date of your graduation! Of course I told Geoffrey that he hadn't a hope of winning in any case; I don't even think they'd let you stay in law school until 2041. My guess is Mother will win the pot; I'm sure she came the *closest to the correct year. That's probably why she's gloating about your newly elevated status. A partner, indeed! Reading between the lines of Mother's propaganda, I deduced that you did not get hired by a real law firm and are therefore striking it out on your own to chase ambulances and draw up wills in the unsuspecting city of Danville, Virginia.*

As I recall, your graduation gift to me in days gone by was an IOU, which I could with perfect justice return to you on the present occasion, but I am more gracious than you (also more solvent), and so enclosed you will find a check for five hundred dollars, which I hope you will use to buy a desk or other bits of office furniture for your new establishment, but if you'd rather buy a thousand baseball cards or a collection of Perry Mason videos to instruct you in trial procedure or whatever else takes your fancy, then you have my blessing. (Seriously, Bill, we are all very happy for you. Keep me posted about your most exciting cases. If you can afford the overseas postal rates.)

No doubt you are all aquiver to learn how your baby sister is doing in the capitals of Europe. Well, the capital of Scotland, anyhow. And the answer is: very well, thank you. Cameron is back from the high seas and he's keeping busy with his flippered friends at the lab while I am attempting to put my Ph.D. in forensic anthropology to some practical use, short of grave-robbing—a time-honored profession in Edinburgh, as you doubtless know. The way Cousin Geoffrey keeps going on about Burke and Hare, you'd think he had stock in the company.

In conclusion, I have just one teensy question about this new law practice of yours. Mother says in her letter that you have gone into partnership with A. P. Hill, which is charming for both of you, I'm sure, except that I had the distinct impression that A. P. Hill had been dead for a hundred and twenty-seven years. I take it, then, that you are the junior partner? I await your explanation of this phenomenon with bated breath.

May you please the Court,
Elizabeth

"Letter from my sister," said Bill MacPherson to his new law partner, the aforementioned A. P. Hill. "I thought you might like to read it. I've already cashed the check, though."

A. P. Hill scanned the letter without a trace of a smile. "*Dead for a hundred and twenty-seven years.* People always say that when they hear my name."

"Surely not *always*," murmured Bill. "There are probably scads of Yankees who don't recognize it at all. Anyway, if it bothers you, you could always use your first name. Amy Hill is a perfectly good name."

"Amy Hill isn't auspicious enough for a practicing attorney," she said, frowning.

"How about using your middle name? Powell is okay. And it's what your folks call you, isn't it?"

His partner shrugged. "Only because I refuse to let anyone call me Amy. I just think initials have a more aggressive and professional sound. Especially for someone as harmless looking as I am."

Bill observed his partner appraisingly. She was just over five feet tall, with short straw-colored hair and the sort of angelic face that necessitated the showing of her ID card rather oftener than most people her age were required to do. "You do put one in mind of a high school cheerleader," Bill conceded. "At first glance, I mean. For those who haven't seen your pit-bull tactics in trial class. But that gleam of blood lust in your green eyes ought to tip off anybody who's paying attention. I expect you come by it honestly, what with all those cavalry charges in your bloodlines."

Bill was referring to the original A. P. Hill, one of Robert E. Lee's generals during the Civil War. The present bearer of that name was the warrior's great-great-granddaughter, who had chosen to fight her battles in court rather than at the head of an army. The family resemblance was there, though, in her no-nonsense manner and in the easy self-confidence that she displayed in legal combat. Her grades in law school had been better than Bill's, and he still marveled at his good fortune that she had agreed to go into partnership with him. He was sure she could have snared a lucrative position in an established law firm if she'd wanted one. But she said that if she didn't strike out on her own, the family would make her practice law with her cousin Stinky. She wanted to make it through her own efforts, she said, without family influence.

Bill had never met his law partner's family, but he knew that she came from somewhere west of Roanoke, and, although she didn't speak of it, he could well imagine a rural law practice in southwest Virginia, replete with drunk drivers and bad-check cases. There would already be a couple of well-established attorneys there who would get all the business, leaving newcomers to scramble for the lowest-paying leftovers. Here in Danville there was at least a chance of some criminal cases, which were A.P.'s specialty, and a population of sufficient size to provide them with the more prosaic legal business of wills and no-fault divorces, which would generate most of the revenue for the firm of two.

Fortunately their rent was modest. The newly graduated lawyers had set up headquarters downtown in an old bank building which now housed a florist shop, a travel agency, and a number of small apartments on the two upper floors, one of which had also been rented by Bill MacPherson, because it was the cheapest accommodation he could find. A.P., who preferred to see criminals in court rather than in the stairwell of her building, had moved into a more secure and luxurious high rise on the outskirts of town.

The law office consisted of three small rooms partitioned with wallboard out of one large one—on the landlord's theory that three rabbit hutches ought to rent for more than one decent-sized room. The frosted glass door opened into a reception area, containing as yet no secretary. On either side of this waiting room, doors led to the tiny offices of Bill MacPherson and A. P. Hill, each furnished with a secondhand desk and bookcase, law books, a typewriter, and very little else. The new attorneys had their independence, an optimism that might pass for recklessness in more conservative circles, and less than a thousand dollars to get on with. Business had better become brisk very soon.

"So, partner, how was your morning?" Bill asked.

"All right, I guess," said A. P. Hill. "I went down to the courthouse and introduced myself around. I put my name on the list of attorneys who can be assigned to court-appointed cases. How did things go here?"

"Crowd control wasn't a problem. I called the business college to see if we could get a part-time secretary that we could afford. They're sending over an applicant this afternoon."

"Good," said A.P. "I'll interview her. You'd fall for the first hard-luck story you heard, without bothering to find out if she could type."

"Well, ask her if she suffers from claustrophobia." He looked at the walls, little more than an arm's length away. "It could be a liability in this office."

"This is what we can afford," said A.P. "If we don't get some business soon, we may be operating out of a packing crate on the sidewalk."

"Probably against city ordinances," said Bill. "I would offer to go and chase an ambulance, but unless I get my car tuned up, I probably couldn't catch one."

A.P. glanced again at Elizabeth's letter. "At least we got some more money. I hope you remember to thank your sister for this."

"It's high on my list of things to do this afternoon," Bill promised. He held up a cardboard box. "Speaking of that check, I also got a little something to brighten up the office. I went out to deposit the check from my sister, and as I was coming back, I happened to look into that flea-market place . . . I'll just put it on the table in the corner." He took his newly purchased prize out of its wrappings of newspaper and set it on the white plastic table scrounged from Goodwill. "What do you think?"

"I think it's dead," said A. P. Hill. "Did you actually pay money for that monstrosity?"

"Yes. Elizabeth suggested that I spend the money on office furniture, but when I saw this fellow here at the flea market, I just had to have him."

"What flea market?"

"That store down on the corner. I think it used to be a grocery store, but now some antique dealers have set up stalls inside. So, anyhow, I went in, just out of curiosity—"

"Do they have any old weapons in there? Swords, things like that?"

"I didn't notice," said Bill. "Probably. The place is full of junk. Why?"

"Oh, no reason. So you found this dead animal in drag—"

"The taxidermist says that he's an authentic Virginia groundhog. And he wasn't killed for display. He's a road kill," Bill added happily. "And his little black robe is handmade by the taxidermist's wife. Isn't he marvelous?"

A. P. Hill frowned into the leering face of a large marmot, who was stuffed and mounted in a standing position. Moreover, it was dressed in a black satin gown that might have been judge's robes or graduation attire. "Hmm. I don't suppose it occurred to you to buy a filing cabinet or two instead? Maybe some office supplies?"

"Oh, there's enough money left over for that," Bill assured her. "Especially if we buy secondhand stuff. But this fellow was too wonderful to pass up. He's one of a kind. I thought we'd call him Flea Bailey. Get it? Like F. Lee—"

"Yes, well. Keep him in your office, okay, Bill?"

Bill remained cheerful and unoffended at this dismissal of his prize. "I thought I would," he agreed. "After all, you've got a mascot of your own, haven't you?" He pointed to a Lucite paperweight on the otherwise empty desk. Embedded in the clear plastic was a round bit of bone, like the center shank in a slice of country ham.

"It's a present from my folks," said A.P. "Family tradition. When the original A. P. Hill went off to join the Confederacy, his mother gave him a ham bone as a good-luck piece. He kept it with him all through the war."

"And that's why he made it through safely, you think?"

"Well, no," said the general's namesake. "Actually, he was shot by Union soldiers in 1865 and didn't survive the war. My great-grandmother was born a couple of months after he died. But he was a hell of a general, so I guess my folks figured it might inspire me to greatness in the law."

"If they'd throw a little business our way, that wouldn't hurt either," Bill pointed out.

His partner shrugged. "Cousin Stinky takes care of most of the family's legal stuff. But maybe our newspaper ad will bring us clients."

There was a knock at the door, and a well-dressed woman came in, carrying a beribboned potted plant.

"There!" said A. P. Hill triumphantly. "A client already! Unless you're here to interview for the secretary's job?"

"Neither, I'm afraid," said Bill MacPherson. "Hello, Mom."

As she set the housewarming gift on the secretary's desk, Margaret MacPherson managed a tight smile. "Hello, sweetheart," she said, hugging her son. "Actually, I *am* a client. Bill, could I see you in private?"

◆   ◆   ◆

A. P. HILL SPENT the next couple of minutes profusely apologizing to her partner's mother, whom she had met briefly at graduation, but had not recognized in the present instance. Their exchange of pleasantries was cordial but strained. Margaret Chandler MacPherson looked anxious, as if she could hardly keep her mind on the conversation. Inventing urgent tasks to attend to, A.P. retired to her office, leaving Bill to confer with his distracted relative. In her clean but spartan office, A.P. sat in her swivel chair for all of one minute before restlessness overtook her. Then she dusted a spotless desk, adjusted books that were perfectly straight, and resharpened all her pencils. Pride did not come cheap, she thought, looking around the shabby office with its threadbare green carpet and its battered old desk.

With her grades and family connections, she could have taken a job at any number of prestigious law firms in Richmond or northern Virginia. There the offices would have been considerably grander, but that would have meant working for the Silverbacks, as she liked to call them. She'd found *Silverback* in a *National Geographic* article on gorillas. It was the term used for the large, overbearing males who attempted to dominate the group, and right away she recognized the similarity between gorilla troops and law firms.

Her new partner, Bill MacPherson, although large and male, was definitely not a Silverback. He would be hard put to dominate anything more assertive than goldfish, but he was reasonably competent, rather good-looking once you got used to him, and unfailingly even-tempered and amiable. For someone who considered coffee one of the four major food groups, the contrast of Bill's placid temperament was invaluable; it counteracted her own tendencies toward anxiety and overwork. The legal world might see William D. MacPherson as the crucial member of the team, the presentable young male eligible for membership in the old-boy network, but A. P. Hill knew for a fact it was her talent and ambition that would make the firm succeed; Bill was along for decoration and emotional ballast, and because her one weakness was a genuine affection for hopeless innocents. Somebody had to see that he didn't starve, she told herself.

Besides, A.P. had a hobby that was more or less a secret, and she didn't want the pressure and visibility of a high-profile law firm. There's no telling who might see you there. Sleepy little Danville was both convenient and private for her extracurricular activities.

When the telephone rang, A.P. considered posing as the secretary they didn't have, but she couldn't figure out how then to take the call as her real self, so she abandoned pretense and said into the receiver: "MacPherson and Hill. A. P. Hill speaking."

"Yes," said a woman's voice. "I saw the announcement in the paper that you had just opened for business, so I thought I'd give you a call. I need something rather unusual in the way of legal services."

A. P. Hill glanced apprehensively in the direction of her law books. "Could you be more specific?" she ventured.

"Well, I'd like to put an attorney on retainer as a birthday gift to my husband." The woman laughed. "My name is Frances Trowbridge. I know it may sound strange to give your husband a lawyer as a present, and of course he has legal representatives for his business, but this is different."

"Is it a personal problem?" asked A.P., still puzzled.

"It certainly is! He's driving me crazy. My husband is a born complainer, you see, and he's always fuming about something—wanting to know if it's legal. Suppose we're out in the car, for instance, and he sees a policeman drive by in a patrol car. If the policeman has a cigarette in his hand, Calvin will want to know if it's legal for policemen to smoke while on duty. Or he'll wonder if the taxpayers will have to pay for repairs to the seat covers if the policeman burns holes in the car's upholstery. Well, there's no use asking *me* things like that. I'm no more of a lawyer than Calvin is, but that doesn't stop him from droning on about it until I could scream. So finally—I mean, I have put up with this for *years*—I hit upon a possible solution. I want to hire an attorney for one year to look up every one of Calvin's stupid questions."

"So, as I understand it, you wish to put us on retainer to research legal questions for Mr. Trowbridge." A. P. Hill was making notes on a yellow legal pad.

"Exactly! So if Calvin suddenly wants to know if he can make a citizen's arrest of someone taking up two parking spaces at the mall, he can call you, instead of boring me with it. You can look it up for him, give him a precise legal answer, and he'll be happy. Can you do that for a yearly flat fee?"

It wasn't as if there were any other cases demanding their undivided attention. "Well," said A.P., "what if we gave you fifty questions a year for a flat fee, and then billed you for anything over that amount?"

Mrs. Trowbridge considered the offer. "That ought to be about right," she declared. "Once a week is about as often as he gets a real bee in his bonnet. The rest of his quibbles are things he'll forget five minutes later. And some of them probably won't take you any research at all. Can you do it for $2,500?"

Visions of rent receipts danced in her head. "Yes, Mrs. Trowbridge," said A. P. Hill. "My partner Bill—er, Mr. MacPherson—will be delighted to handle the matter for you. Why don't you come in later to work out the details? We can type up a document for you to give Mr. Trowbridge on his birthday."

◆　◆　◆

SHE WAS STILL TINKERING with the rough draft of the Trowbridge agreement when Bill MacPherson walked in, looking like a clairvoyant on the deck of the *Titanic*.

"Has your mother gone already?" A.P. asked him, still intent upon her work. When there was no reply, she looked up. "What's the matter, Bill?"

"Got my first case," he said woodenly. "I tried to talk her out of it, of course, but she insisted."

"What is it?"

Bill managed a bitter smile. "Apparently," he said, "I am handling my mother's divorce proceedings."

A.P. set the pen down and stared at his stricken face. "Not an example of your family's bizarre sense of humor?" she ventured.

"I thought of that. 'A little lawyer humor to brighten up the old office-warming?' I said cheerily to Mother. But she gave me that look that I haven't seen since Elizabeth and I used Miss Clairol on the cat, so I think we can assume that she is not joking. Imagine the surprise of the only son, yours truly. I mean, they've been married nearly thirty years. You'd think they'd be resigned to one another by now."

"I've heard that men get strange once they pass fifty," said A.P. thoughtfully. "They seem to want loud plaid jackets and sports cars the size of roller skates. I suppose that the old wife doesn't fit the new image."

"Mother was rather vague about that," said Bill. "I gather that something pretty disastrous has transpired at home. Lipstick on the collar, perhaps. Anyway, the old girl's gone ballistic. She wants me to file the papers right away, ask for alimony, and generally take poor Dad to the cleaners."

"I don't think that handling divorces within one's own family is such a good idea, Bill."

"I know! And I said so like a shot! But then she misted up on me, said she supposed one couldn't trust *any* man if her own son wouldn't even come to her defense in her time of need. She went on in that vein until I was ready to disembowel myself with the tape dispenser. Finally I just said I would represent her. I'd have said anything by that time. Probably have chipped in for a hit man if she'd asked me to."

A. P. Hill shook her head. "You must learn to be firm with people, Bill. Besides, didn't it occur to you to recommend counseling before they break up a decades-old marriage?"

"She wouldn't hear of it. Said something like, '*I'm* not the one who needs professional help!' " He groaned. "I suppose I'd better review the stuff we have on divorce procedures."

"You have a client coming in this afternoon. I was just drafting the agreement." Briefly she told him about Mrs. Trowbridge and her querulous husband.

"She's putting us on retainer?" said Bill. "Let me get this straight. Mr. Trowbridge asks whatever silly questions he wants and I root around in the law books and come up with an answer for him."

"Right."

"And he doesn't want to sue or press charges against offenders or anything like that? He just wants to know—for his own satisfaction?"

"Apparently so."

"And she's *paying* us for that?"

"Fifty dollars per question. In advance. Almost the whole year's rent." A.P. permitted herself a triumphant smile. "I'll just go and type this up so that we'll be ready when she gets here. Don't forget to write to your sister and thank her for the check."

"My sister!" cried Bill. "You'd better believe I'm going to write her!"

"Share the bad news, huh?" said A.P. "How do you think she'll take it?"

"You know that legal phrase *in loco parentis*?"

"Yes. And that's not what it means at all."

"It ought to," muttered Bill. "It describes her perfectly."

◆　◆　◆

We don't know how it started
But they've invaded us now and we're bound to fight
Till every last damn Yankee goes home and quits.
We used to think we could lick them in one hand's turn.
We don't think that any more.

—STEPHEN VINCENT BENÉT,
John Brown's Body, Book 4

RICHMOND—APRIL 2, 1865

GABRIEL HAWKS RECKONED he wasn't in the navy anymore. It was amazing how fast a peaceful afternoon could turn into a foretaste of hell. He still hadn't taken it all in. After the admiral had given the order to sail the fleet up to the signal station at Drewry's Bluff, there had been scarcely time to think. The sailors had been like ants scurrying around the ship, almost knocking one another over in their haste to get things done. And there was a strained silence to the work, not like the usual bustle on board when the men chaffed one another and larked about as they worked. Now they communed with their thoughts and hurried through the tasks, tight-lipped and pale. It seemed that the end was coming, and while it hadn't exactly been a surprise, it was still a shock to find that the inconceivable had come to pass. They were retreating. Richmond would fall.

They brought the provisions out of the hold and began to hand them out in packages, one to each member of the crew. These were rations to last who knew how long as they journeyed to who knew where. Suddenly Gabe had more food than he'd seen in weeks, but he wasn't hungry anymore. His stomach felt like a bucket of James River water. The men gathered up their few personal possessions, unlashing hammocks and scrounging for canteens and blankets, muttering all the while among themselves about what this might mean.

"We're for it now," declared one grizzled veteran of the seas. "You know what this means, don't you?"

Some of the younger crewmen, impressed for duty from army regiments, looked bug-eyed with fright, just like Gabe felt. "What's it mean?" asked one.

"Why—defeat!" roared the old salt. "I reckon we'll all be civilians come morning. And then we better get 'way from here quick as we can, lest we all be shot! By the Federals! Oh, they're a-coming all right. You just watch the sky, boys, and you'll see."

Sure enough, not five minutes after he'd made this prediction, as they were up on deck stowing their gear away as best they could, somebody shouted, "Lookee yonder!" They turned the way he was pointing to see the whole sky on the north side of the James aglow with the fires of Richmond.

"It's the Yankees, come from Petersburg!" someone called out.

But an officer nearby overheard, and he said, "Not yet it isn't, boys. That's our soldiers burning what they can't take with them before they head south. That'll be materiel and barracks going up in smoke."

"What's going to happen to us, sir?"

The officer scowled as if he didn't want to answer, but finally he replied. "You'll be boarding one of the wooden gunships for now. That's all you need to be told."

Tom Bridgeford leaned over and whispered to Gabe. "You think there's any chance of making a run for it?"

Gabe looked up at the orange sky over Richmond. He shook his head. "It wouldn't be fittin' to run away," he said. "Besides, doesn't look like there's too awful many places to go."

It was well past midnight when the crew of the ironclads were finally provisioned and allowed to board one of the fleet's five wooden gunboats. Gabe and Tom Bridgeford found themselves wedged together on the deck of the *Roanoke*, their faces illuminated by the glare from the burning ironclads. Admiral Semmes had ordered that the ships be torched rather than left to fall into the hands of the enemy.

"He could have just scuttled them," said Gabe, watching the flames dance across the deck of the *Virginia*.

"Maybe he thought that time was getting short," said Bridgeford. "Besides, what's one more fire in the midst of this conflagration?" He pointed toward the sky over Richmond, still bright with the evidence of the night's destruction.

"What do you think is going to happen now?" asked Gabe.

"Depends on how Lee has fared in Petersburg," said Bridgeford. "If he still has fight in him, we might move the government south and keep fighting. Charleston would make a nice capital. Or Wilmington."

"But we're going upriver," Gabe said.

Bridgeford stared off at the dancing fire shapes, pretending he hadn't heard. Gabe wondered what he ought to do now. Pa could sure use him at home for the farm work this time of year, and it didn't look like the Confederacy had much longer to live, but still he didn't feel right about leaving just because things were going bad. If you gave your word on something, you stuck it out.

The *Roanoke*, moving steadily upriver, away from the burning ironclads, had not gone more than a quarter of a mile before an explosion shook the water, making the vessel lurch to starboard and tremble like a sapling in a hurricane. The flames had reached the ironclad's magazine, whose loaded shells had not been removed by the departing crew. When the shell room exploded, it lit the shells' fuses and catapulted the live ammunition high into the air above the river, giving the navy a send-off of spectacular fireworks. But no one cheered.

The ships endured an hour's wait at one of the drawbridges between Richmond and Drewry's Bluff, while the troops who had set the evening's bonfires were allowed passage across the bridge. The route they had taken was punctuated with patches of leaping flames as the Confederates—literally—burned their bridges behind them. While the sailors were waiting for the span to be raised, the sky began to go from black to gray, and finally first light gave them a glimpse of the devastation.

Whole city blocks were now ablaze, and the Tredegar Iron Works flamed like hell itself, rending the morning air with the shudders of the exploding shells within it. A dense cloud of smoke hung over the city, like a blanket laid over a corpse. There wouldn't be much left for the Yankees to take now, and the people of Richmond knew it. A great throng of them were gathered on the Manchester side of the river, trying to escape the conflagration.

The gunboat docked, and the men of the James River fleet tumbled ashore, weighted down with all their belongings, too stunned from the rush of disasters to think what to do next.

"I hope they don't expect us to march any considerable distance," said Bridgeford. "Most of us couldn't do more than a couple of miles at the best of times, not being used to it."

"I reckon I can walk," said Gabe Hawks. "I followed Stonewall from one end of Virginia to t'other. But I ain't no damn pack mule."

"Ah, Hawks, but at the moment you look like one." Bridgeford laughed and pointed to the jumble of necessities they carried: a mess-kettle, bags of bread, chunks of salted pork, pots and pans, tea, sugar, and tobacco. Which of these precious items could they leave behind in their flight? And what would become of them if they did not?

"Hey, you old salts! How do you like navigating on land?" A line of cavalry was passing by on the road—boys scarcely older than Gabe, looking thin and tired in their tattered gray. But when they saw the grounded sailors, staggering about on dry land with pans around their necks, like a gaggle of stranded geese, they cheered up considerably, and drifted out of sight still laughing and making catcalls at their less fortunate comrades in arms.

Admiral Semmes, without a ship under him, looked just as lost as anyone. He gave orders for the gunboats to be burned and set adrift. Then he called on his captains to muster the troops. Only now the captains were to be called colonels.

"My orders are to join General Lee in the field with all my forces!" the admiral called out. "And we shall proceed accordingly."

Bridgeford nudged Gabe and said softly, "But where the devil is Lee, and how do we get there?"

Just then one of the officers shouted, "To the railroad depot! Forward, march!"

And they lurched off into a cloud of smoke and road dust.

Gabriel Hawks had just rejoined the army.

Newtown, Edinburgh

Dear Bill,

If I hadn't received a terse (and utterly incomprehensible) letter from Mother on the same day your note arrived, I would not have dreamed of believing you. In fact, I would have been appalled at your lack of taste and judgment in perpetrating such a prank, and I might have considered giving your name to every insurance salesman in Danville, just to keep you occupied for a bit as unpleasantly as possible. But apparently it is true. Mother and Daddy are getting a divorce. I still haven't fully grasped it. I suppose it would be useless asking them to stay together for the sake of the children when both of us have postgraduate degrees? But still!

I feel as if I'd just fallen off a tightrope and there is no longer any safety net beneath me. I suppose that family is one of those things that people simply take for granted. Or maybe I stopped thinking of Mother and Daddy as people with new experiences ahead of them. To me they just were, *like Mount Rushmore or Old Faithful. They weren't supposed to change. I was the one who was allowed to go off and have adventures. They were supposed to be the one constant in my life. I don't like this new world one bit. Can we put it back the way it was? Did you try?*

I tried calling home about six times, but Mother is being brittle and maddeningly perky. "These things happen." "Of course we'll always be friends." You know the sort of rot people speak when they don't want to tell you what's really going on. I didn't want to push it. And I called Daddy at his office and got much the same line, except in a more dignified and forbidding tone.

I know you think I'm going to be on the next plane to Richmond, but I can't. I have job interviews coming up here and I simply can't get away.

Anyhow, divorces take months and months, so I suppose there's no real rush. Perhaps we ought to let them simmer down a bit before we do any meddling. But meanwhile you must try to find out what's going on! We can't deal with this thing until we know the facts. Tell Mother that as her attorney you have to be told everything. *And keep me posted. I mean* often.

Bill, I'm relying on you. You're the family's only hope. Don't let this happen!

Love,
Elizabeth

"A few more days for to tote the weary load"
— STEPHEN FOSTER,
"My Old Kentucky Home"

CHAPTER

2

"I'M NOT GOING to be here this afternoon," said A. P. Hill. "Can you manage by yourself?"

"By myself?" Bill MacPherson looked up from his paperwork. "You mean alone? Abandoned? What about Edith?"

"Try to bear up, Bill. It's Edith's day off, remember? Tuesday afternoons and all day Friday."

The law firm of MacPherson and Hill was now ten days old, still solvent, and boasted a caseload of half a dozen clients. They had also engaged a part-time secretary-receptionist: Edith Creech, a recent graduate of the local business college. Edith's salary was as modest as her grade point average. She was maddeningly slow at office work and her spelling showed a creativity that bordered on genius, but she was a notary public, a useful asset to a law firm, and she was thoroughly in awe of her attorney employers, which went a long way toward offsetting her shortcomings.

"And where are you going this afternoon?" Bill wanted to know.

A. P. Hill reddened. "I've got an appointment," she said, in a tone calculated to discourage further inquiry. "But you should be all right. Have you heard from Trowbridge yet?"

"Yep. He called this morning with his first question. It's a doozy. Are you ready for this? He wants to know: if a neighbor's tomcat gets the Trowbridge tabby in the family way, can the tomcat's owner be sued for child—er, kitten—support?"

His partner rolled her eyes. "Oh, just say no!" she advised.

"That's easy for *you* to say, Powell," Bill grumbled. "You're a Republican. But Old Trowbridge wants chapter and verse. I did inform him that the kittens would have to have blood tests to prove paternity."

"Well, I'm sure you'll come up with something. Did you remember to check the mail before you came in?"

"Yes. That's the other thing I was going to tell you about. You know that newspaper ad we ran? Did we say that we were catering in legal services to the deranged or anything?"

"Why?"

"They seem to be seeking us out. First the Trowbridges and now this." He held up a flowered envelope. "This letter came today, addressed to us—MacPherson and Hill, Attorneys at Law. *Dear Sirs: If it is entirely convenient with you, I shall be calling on Friday afternoon at one o'clock to discuss a small legal matter in which I should like to avail myself of your services. Sincerely, Flora Dabney.* And—get this, Powell—Miss Dabney has enclosed a picture of herself in costume."

"Let me see that!" A. P. Hill snatched the picture from her partner's outstretched hand. From the sepia photograph a lovely but earnest-looking young woman gazed back at her with big, intelligent eyes. Flora Dabney looked a proper Edwardian gentlewoman in her coat with wide lapels and a frilled blouse with a jabot of lace at her throat. Her dark hair was brushed away from her forehead and tied with a ribbon at the back, a style that eschewed glamour, but did not hide her wholesome good looks.

"I think I'm in love," said Bill.

"She looks too intelligent for you," said A.P., handing back the photograph. "She doesn't say what she wants?"

"No. Women seem determined to be mysterious in my presence. Where are *you* going this afternoon, by the way?"

His partner smiled sweetly. "Just out. Now try not to do anything that will get you disbarred."

Bill was still laughing merrily as A.P. left the office. She glanced at her watch. Nearly one o'clock. Just as well that she'd packed her gear this morning. She hated to leave the car parked downtown with the rifle in the trunk, but it couldn't be helped. Now she had to go into the ladies' room and change. It wouldn't do to show up in her present outfit: a pink linen coat and skirt and high heels. Better stow them in a locked briefcase in the trunk, just to be safe, after she changed into her other set of clothes.

Anyone loitering about on the sidewalk in front would have insisted that A. P. Hill did not leave the building that afternoon. However, a teenaged boy in a hat and overcoat might have been observed leaving the second-floor ladies' room with a briefcase.

◆　◆　◆

AN HOUR LATER Bill was still attempting to make sense of the vagaries of feline paternity when an elderly woman appeared in the outer office. She wore a black silk dress and pearls and she had posture that a general would envy. She took in her surroundings in one piercing glance. But when she saw Bill peering at her through the open door of his office, her demeanor changed to one of fluffy amiability. She smiled as she came in, motioning for him to sit back down.

"A. P. Hill?" she said eagerly.

"No, ma'am. She's my partner, but she's not here right now. And our secretary's gone, too. I'm Bill MacPherson."

The woman in black surveyed Bill's shabby surroundings. Her sharp eyes flickered over the framed diploma and the secondhand furniture.

They paused momentarily on the gaily appareled rodent leering at her from the corner.

"I think you'll do fine," she declared, settling happily into the captain's chair Bill had purchased from Goodwill for the comfort of his clients. "I thought I'd drop by today because Lydia had to come downtown anyway to do her incessant courthouse research. I just know she drives them all crazy down there in the records office. Tracing her family tree, you know. She can't quite prove a connection between her people and Robert E. Lee, so now she's trying to find out the maternal grandmother of the man he bought Traveller from!"

Bill blinked, trying to find his way into the conversation.

"That's why we thought it would be such fun to have A. P. Hill as an attorney. She might know something about the general's family connections that the Danville Courthouse doesn't have a record of." She stopped herself, as if she had just realized that the young man might see this preference as a personal slight. "But of course our legal business has nothing to do with the war at all," she hastened to explain. "It's just a simple little old transaction. I bet you could do it standing on your head."

Bill pictured Mr. Trowbridge bursting in and shouting, "Is it legal for an attorney to plead a case while standing on his head?" He smiled and ventured a question of his own. "Were we expecting you this afternoon, ma'am?"

Her gray eyes widened in surprise. "Why, I hope so, young man! I took the trouble to write you."

Bill began to shuffle through the papers on his desk when she leaned over and announced, "There! You have my picture right there on top of your desk calendar." She pointed one white-gloved finger at the sepia portrait of the Edwardian beauty.

Bill stared from one to the other. "You . . . I mean to say . . . Is that—"

She nodded with a satisfied little smile. "Oh, yes! It's me all right. A good many years ago, before I married Mr. Dabney, rest his soul. My name is Flora."

"But why did you send me this picture?"

Flora Dabney took a deep breath. "Well, young man, I'll tell you. I get rather tired of being dismissed as *just* an old lady, so I thought I'd make a proper first impression on you. Just so you'd know who I really am, underneath this sixty years of erosion."

Bill smiled. "I wish I'd known you then."

The old lady's eyes twinkled. "I expect I'd have led you a pretty dance, Mr. MacPherson. Now let us get to the matter at hand. My friends and I would like you to sell our house. It's a lovely old colonial with Corinthian columns, ten bedrooms, fireplaces—"

"Mrs. Dabney! Whoa! Wait! Stop. I'm really sorry, ma'am. You're a little confused. You see, I'm a lawyer, not a real estate agent. But if you'd like me to find you one . . ." He reached for the telephone book.

"We don't want a realtor," she said, motioning for him to put the book away. "We need a lawyer. You see, there are only eight of us left and the house is just too big. The upkeep is very expensive, so we thought we'd see about selling it."

"Eight of you own a house?" Bill's mind was reeling at the legal intricacies of such a transaction.

"It amounts to that," said Flora Dabney. "There is a deed of something or other, leaving the house to the widows and daughters of Confederate veterans."

"A deed of trust? A deed of covenant?"

"Yes," said Flora Dabney, as if the two were interchangeable, which they certainly were in Bill's mind, because he could not remember the details of that particular law class.

"You want to sell the Home for Confederate Widows?" asked Bill.

"Women," Flora Dabney corrected him. "There are only eight of us widows and daughters left."

Bill did a rapid mental calculation. The Civil War had ended one hundred and twenty-something years ago. Surely the supply of widows and daughters must have run out. "How could there still be eight of you left after all these years?"

"We are the daughters of men who fought in the War as boys and who married quite late in life. My father was fourteen when he ran off to join the Confederacy. My mother was his third wife, whom he married in 1920, when he was seventy and she was twenty-three. My memories of him are quite dim by now, of course. The only actual widow is—"

"And the eight of you want to sell the home? Can you do that?"

"Yes. The deed says we can. You see, the house was bequeathed to the female dependents of Confederate veterans by a Colonel Phillips. He was a Confederate colonel, you see, and the house used to be his. It dates from before the War."

Bill didn't bother to ask Miss Dabney which war. As far as she was concerned, there hadn't been another one. So the house was about a hundred and fifty years old. He'd have to go and take a look at it.

"Colonel Phillips was a generous man," Flora was saying. "But he was nobody's fool. Of course when he was drawing up the terms of the gift, he realized that sooner or later there would be no more dependents to benefit from his bequest. So it says—after a lot of *wherefores* and suchlike lawyerly talk—that when the trustees of the house feel that it is no longer needed, they may dispose of the property as they see fit. And, young man, the trustees of the house are the residents themselves!"

"And you want to sell it?"

"Yes. As I said, the upkeep is high, and there is far too much space for us. Not to mention the stairs. We talked it over and decided that we'd like to go to a nice retirement home just outside of town, so we'd like to arrange for a private sale of the property."

"Doesn't the foundation—or whatever it is—have an attorney already?"

Flora Dabney sighed prettily. "He passed away, poor thing. And he was only seventy."

"Surely a realtor—"

"No. We talked about that. Because the house is quite old and valuable, we decided that we could get a better price for it if we did not try to sell it locally." She beamed at their collective cleverness. "So we thought we could have you run an ad in one of those papers up North. *The New York Times*, perhaps. And we'd see if we could get some wealthy Northerner to purchase it because it wouldn't seem so expensive to him, house prices being what they are up there."

"You want to sell the Home to a Yankee?" gasped Bill.

Flora Dabney favored him with a pitying smile. "Mr. MacPherson," she said gently, "the War is over."

◆ ◆ ◆

UNFORTUNATELY AT THE HOME of Bill's parents, the war was far from over. Bill spent the rest of an uneventful afternoon after Flora Dabney's departure listening to the sound of a phone *not* ringing—and dreading his evening dinner engagement: one final meal with Mother and Dad at the old homeplace, after which he would stay the night in order to help Dad move out in the morning.

Without his legal assistance, Bill's parents had come to the decision that Margaret MacPherson would keep the house. Doug MacPherson would move to an apartment within close commuting distance of his office. He was going to take some of the family furniture with him, but there was still some debate between them as to what would go and what would stay. Bill kept asking who was getting custody of his baby pictures and his Little League trophies, but his parents seemed unconcerned with these major issues, preferring to squabble over record albums and cookware. Really, he thought, there was no accounting for some people's sense of values. They weren't being exactly forthcoming about the cause of the breakup, either, and he hardly liked to press the matter, because he found it all hideously embarrassing. He wasn't even sure he wanted to know. For legal purposes they were attributing the estrangement to *irreconcilable differences*, which is legalspeak for "none of your business." He knew one thing, though—it wasn't a friendly divorce, if, indeed, such a thing exists.

As Bill drove the sunny country road from Danville to the MacPherson home in Franklin County, he was hounded by a succession of infelicitous images of the evening to come. *Pork Chop Hill*: he is caught between his parents in a ruthless food fight. *Medea:* Mother decides that poison is much tidier than legal proceedings and spikes the pot roast with strychnine; they all die together. *Get the Guest:* they hold an inquest on their marriage and decide that their incompatibility is all *his* fault; his grades and his table manners are mentioned.

Bill groaned aloud. This was not how he imagined his first months of law practice. Attorneys were supposed to have seamy and depressing legal cases while their private lives were happy and carefree. But with him—just the reverse! He had a cheery little practice answering *Jeop-*

ardy questions and helping little old ladies while his private life was shot to hell.

He should have asked A. P. Hill to take his parents' case. Okay, he should have begged harder. But when they first agreed to go into practice together, Powell had declared that she would rather starve than take divorce cases, and Bill had agreed that he'd handle those should the occasion arise. So there he was, stuck with the family civil war, while Powell enjoyed herself at the courthouse, hobnobbing with car thieves and burglars, leaving him to do the dirty work.

When he noticed that the landmarks were becoming familiar, he came out of his reverie with a heavy heart. Only a few miles left to go before he entered the war zone. Over the bridge, up the hill past the Hudson's Christmas tree farm, and then he'd see the stone pillars that led into Chancellorsville Estates. His parents' colonial brick home was on Mead Lane, a winding blacktop that spiraled up the wooded ridge studded with large homes, all carefully different and even more carefully landscaped to blend into the hillside. Bill wished *he* could blend into the hillside. Odd how relationships are embarrassing in any generation but one's own. He was too uncomfortable to contemplate this bit of philosophy, however. Tonight was still going to last about eight months, as far as Bill was concerned. He pulled into the concrete driveway, resisting the temptation to hit a nearby tree, just for the sake of a diversion.

Bill's father came strolling out of the garage, wearing a pained smile that he usually reserved for bad puns and funerals. (Good God! She hadn't locked him out, had she?) Other than that, he looked all right. He seemed a little scruffy in his old blue cardigan and paint-stained khakis, but he didn't look haggard or distraught or anything else that would have sent Bill screaming into the shrubbery.

Bill hauled himself out of the car, feeling like a leper who has found work as a bill collector. "Hullo, Dad," he mumbled, fiddling with his car keys. "How's it going?"

"I can't complain, son." The pained smile reappeared. "It might be expensive."

Bill winced. "Couldn't we call a truce for the evening?"

Doug MacPherson sighed wearily. "I didn't start this, Bill. You'd better clear your cease-fire with her." He nodded toward the silent house. "She's probably watching us from behind the living room curtains, so be careful what you do. Don't laugh or anything, or she'll be after you, too."

"I wish someone would tell me what's going on," Bill muttered. "From Mother I get sound bites. I've heard politicians who were more forthcoming."

"Don't expect me to make sense of it. Your mother says that now that you kids are grown, she wants to find herself. Says she's not being fulfilled. Wants to live her own life. Whose live has she been living up to now? I asked her. That didn't sit well, either."

"Can't she find herself without getting a divorce?" asked Bill. He felt a guilty twinge, knowing that he was discussing his client with the opposing side, but he ignored his lawyerly conscience, telling himself that the parental relationship superceded the legal one. "Can't she just take a course in oil painting at the community college?"

"Apparently not. I suggested something of the sort and she shied one of her tole-painted candlesticks in my direction."

"I'll have a word with her," Bill promised. "I still seem to be in her good graces."

Bill picked up his overnight case and walked toward the front door. As he reached for the doorknob, his mother appeared, eyes blazing. "Having a father-son chat, are we? It's disgusting how you men stick together."

Bill attempted a deprecating laugh. "Oh, no, we were just saying hello, Mother."

Margaret MacPherson's expression did not change. "And did he tell you about his girlfriend?"

Bill MacPherson felt his appetite shrivel away to nothingness. This evening was going to last longer than the Seven Days' Battle.

◆　◆　◆

IN A STATELY WHITE-COLUMNED HOUSE on a country road near Danville, tea was being served. In a formal dining room gleaming with silver and well-polished mahogany, the residents of the Home for Confederate Women were listening to Flora Dabney, punctuating her remarks with the discreet clink of spoons on bone china cups. So intent were they upon her report that when Julia Hotchkiss reached for the last slice of date bread, no one contested it.

"I think we've found our lawyer, ladies," Flora Dabney was saying. "I think he'll do quite well by us." She took a tentative sip of her tea, then added another dollop of milk.

"Has he agreed to sell the house?" asked Ellen Morrison. She seemed even more nervous than usual, and she almost whispered her question, as if she feared Union spies behind the velvet draperies.

Flora's eyes twinkled. "Well, he was a bit reluctant at first, because the transaction sounded so complicated, what with eight owners and all —but I persuaded him that it was a simple transaction, and he has consented to take it on."

"Oh, Flora! Are you sure this is wise?" Mary Lee Pendleton had an expression of such sweetness and serenity that she still looked beautiful at eighty-one. She loved to wear her fur coat to the shopping mall in hopes of being mistaken for Helen Hayes.

"I'm sure we haven't any choice," Flora Dabney replied. "And as to the wisdom of it, Lydia is supposed to have made sure that all goes well. Does anyone have an alternate suggestion?"

No one did. The others exchanged glances and worried frowns, but no one spoke up. Julia Hotchkiss slurped her tea in the silence, edging her wheelchair closer to the plate of oatmeal cookies when she thought that no one was looking.

"Right. Then I take it we're all in favor of the transaction as it stands?"

"Did you tell him . . . everything?" asked Ellen, glancing nervously about her.

"No, of course I didn't, dear. I simply told him that we wanted to sell our house as expediently as possible. That should be sufficient, I think. He was very sweet, and quite charmed to be helping a dithery old lady like myself."

"And you're sure about this lawyer?" asked Mary.

Flora Dabney smiled. "Oh, yes, dear! He's perfect. An absolute nincompoop. More tea, anyone?"

◆   ◆   ◆

> *Here we go, here we go,*
> *The last parade of the circus-show,*
> *Longstreet's orphans, Lee's everlastin's*
> *Half cast-iron and half corn-pone,*
> *And if gettin' to heaven means prayer and fastin's*
> *We ought to get there on the fasts alone.*
> —STEPHEN VINCENT BENÉT,
> *John Brown's Body,* Book 8

RICHMOND—APRIL 3, 1865

IT HAD SEEMED LIKE a sensible idea at the time: march the
sailors to the railroad depot—and escape from the approaching federal
forces by the fastest and most invincible means of transport: the iron
horse. A southbound train could take them to Danville in a matter of
hours, while the pursuing army would be on the march six days traveling the same distance.

There was but one difficulty with this sterling plan . . .

"It would seem that the Confederacy can add yet another item to its list of shortages," drawled Bridgeford. "We appear to be somewhat lacking in trains, though not, perhaps, in fellow passengers."

The depot was crowded with fleeing civilians and with wounded soldiers who had tottered out of the hospital, bandages and all, to escape the burning capital. The remnants of the Confederate navy clustered together, hemmed in by frightened men and women and crying children. But there were no trains. Only a few unhitched passenger cars into which more refugees had packed themselves, waiting for someone in authority to appear and preside over their deliverance. Admiral Semmes took some of his officers and began to search the train yards. No one challenged their authority. All the railroad workers had run off the previous day, when the last of the trains had departed.

"Where are the trains?" asked Gabriel. He knew the Confederacy had a good supply of railroad cars. Many's the time Stonewall's troops had circled an evening campfire and told the story of Stonewall Jackson and the B&O Railroad. In May 1861, Thomas J. Jackson—then a colonel—and his troops had occupied Harpers Ferry, with more than a hundred miles of Baltimore & Ohio railroad track within the territory he controlled. The B&O was a lifeline for the Union, conveying soldiers and supplies back and forth between Baltimore and the Ohio Valley. Day and night those trains ran, carrying coal and grain to supply the Union and fortify it during the hostilities ahead. Under orders from Richmond, Jackson put up with the incessant trains as long as there was a chance of Maryland seceding to join the Confederacy, but when that hope faded, Jackson was free to take on the B&O. The colonel complained to railroad president John W. Garrett about the endless procession of noisy trains steaming through the narrow river valley, disturbing the nightly slumber of his troops. Mr. Garrett, anxious to keep peace with the occupying army, canceled the night trains so that they would not disturb Colonel Jackson's sleeping soldiers. A few days later, Jackson persuaded the B&O president to reschedule the day trains so as not to interfere with troop maneuvers. Finally *all* the trains were running through Harpers Ferry between the hours of eleven A.M. and one P.M. Was Colonel Thomas J. Jackson satisfied with that? Indeed he was. He promptly sealed off both ends of the valley at Point of Rocks and at Martinsburg, and appropriated fifty-six locomotives and nearly four hundred railroad cars for the Confederacy. His men loved to tell that story around the watch fires. The laughter dulled their hunger.

But where were Stonewall's trains now, in their hour of need?

"Where are the trains?" echoed a steam engineer from the *Fredericksburg*. "Why, I reckon the government's took 'em when they lit out! Hustled away from here yesterday like rats down an anchor chain, and left the rest of us high and dry to face the fire and the Federals."

"He's right!" called out an approaching officer, just back from inspecting the contents of the railroad yard. "There's nothing out there now but a heap of spare parts. And there's one small locomotive, but there's no fire in her, and no railroad men to run her."

"They've left us a locomotive?" roared the steam engineer. "Why, who needs railroad men if they've left us a working engine? I reckon I can run her. Haven't I kept the *Fredericksburg* afloat and sailing all these months? A steam engine is a steam engine, even on land. I say we fire up the damned thing, attach these railroad cars, and make off with it. Who's with me?"

"But what'll we use for fuel?" someone called out. "There's none of that!"

The steam engineer looked around. "I don't reckon the railroad will be needing that there picket fence," he roared. "I say hack her down and throw her in the furnace."

The pall of smoke overhead and the rumble of distant cannons left very little room for argument among the stranded sailors. Anything was better than staying in Richmond. Any gamble was worth taking. As the men surged forward to follow the ship's engineer, they were beset on all sides by the frightened townspeople, begging not to be left behind, but Admiral Semmes ordered them all turned out of the railroad cars.

"It's better for unarmed civilians to fall into the hands of the enemy than for armed soldiers to be left to face them," the admiral told them.

"If our engine will bear the load, we'll take all of you that will fit aboard," an officer promised a sobbing woman. "Once our troops are loaded."

The other commanders were shouting, "Draw the cars together! Couple the cars!"

Gabriel Hawks wondered how long it would take a gang of sailors to assemble a train, and whether it would run if they did succeed in coupling the cars together. Would they be better off slipping away from the station one by one and trying to make it home? Surely the duration of the war could be counted in days. And it was planting time up home in Giles County. It might take him two weeks to walk it, but once he was west of Richmond, he was almost assured of a safe journey back to the mountains. He had been wounded. He had been both a soldier and a sailor. Surely, Gabe thought, he had done all that any government could ask of a man not yet twenty years old. But he looked at the anxious faces of the women, clutching their crying children and regarding the gaggle of sailors with such faith in their own deliverance. He looked at the gaunt cripples from the hospital, hobbling along to help assemble the train. Gabriel cursed himself for a fool, but he followed the throng down to the railroad yard. He knew he couldn't face his family if he ran out on these people now. Besides, his old commander Stonewall was dead; Jeb Stuart was dead; A. P. Hill was dead. Even the ironclad *Virginia* was dead. Who was he to outlive the war?

Tuesday, probably

Dear Bill,

What do you mean, you're drawing up lists of property and assets? Are you out of your mind? Our baby pictures! The green leather chair in the den that we used to fight each other over. How can you hold these possessions hostage in some emotional chess game?

Shouldn't you be trying to talk Mother and Daddy into getting counseling, for heaven's sake? They've been married forever, you know. You can't just help them to throw all that away. And yet, from what I'm hearing, you're docilely filling out your little legal forms and making motions as if these were two total strangers.

Don't you care? Surely you're not so hard up for business that you're going through with this just to keep yourself working! How much are you charging Mother for this, anyhow? And isn't Daddy furious? He did, after all, pay to put you through law school, only to find you used against him in court as a weapon, like an ungrateful trained shark.

None of this makes any sense. But I cannot come over right now. Not that I'm doing all that well with my job interviews. I'm so worried about the family soap opera that I can barely concentrate on the questions. I tried talking about this with Cameron's mother, but she professes to know nothing of such matters. "Fortunately I was widowed," she said. Whatever that means.

Has there ever been a divorce in the family before? I think not! A murderer, yes, but never a divorce.

Please try to be more forthcoming in your future correspondence. It is bad enough to be stuck over here without feeling that things are being kept from me as well.

As well as can be expected,
Elizabeth

"He is tramping out the vintage where the grapes of wrath are stored."

— JULIA WARD HOWE,
"The Battle Hymn of the Republic"

CHAPTER

3

ON MONDAY MORNING Bill stumbled into the office well after nine o'clock, looking like the plaintiff in a hit-and-run case. Edith, ensconced at her receptionist's desk with the morning crossword, studied him silently as he tottered in the doorway.

"You ought to reconsider ambulance chasing," she remarked. "You look like you could stand to catch one." Edith's awe of attorneys had dwindled steadily in the days since she had been hired, a result of close proximity to actual lawyers, who were markedly less omnipotent than she had hitherto supposed. In fact, she would have bet money that she could have beaten both of them in Trivial Pursuit. So much for their fancy university educations.

"I just come to the office to rest," groaned Bill. "My weekend was a nightmare. Have we got any aspirin?"

"Hangover?" asked Edith, looking him over with a practiced eye. Her daddy had been a great one for the bottle and she knew the signs. In Bill's case, though, they seemed to be absent.

"No, but it's only a matter of time," the sufferer assured her. "I spent the weekend in my parents' war zone. Besides, I have a sore back and every muscle in my leg feels like a stretched rubber band. I was helping my dad move the rest of his things out. Same as last weekend. And I think I carried all the heavy stuff."

"Still no chance of a reconciliation?"

"Not on my account. The only thing they seem to agree on is my utter uselessness. Dad won't confide in me because I'm Mother's attorney, and Mother seems convinced that men are in some worldwide conspiracy against women."

"Yeah, I've noticed it myself," said Edith with a trace of a smile.

"So while I wanted to spend the weekend calming them down and infusing some reason into the situation, *they* insisted on spending two days bickering over the furniture. Mother refused to let Dad take a purple and gold tea service that his great-aunt Elinor left them. Mother says she ought to have it because she drinks tea and Dad doesn't."

"That seems reasonable."

"No, it doesn't. In the twenty-odd years that they've owned that tea set, they have never used it, and I know for a fact that Mother hates it. She refuses to admit that now, of course. And I thought we were going to have to call in the U.N. to decide who got the TV with the remote control. I offered to go out and *buy* another clicker, but they ignored me and kept on arguing in that well-bred icy way of theirs. Snide." He mimicked his mother's voice. " 'Of course it's none of my business, Doug, but do you really think you need half the pots and pans, when all you know how to do is microwave TV dinners?' " Bill lowered himself into a chair with a weary groan. "I can't take much more of this. Where's Powell?"

"At the courthouse," said Edith. "She's got another case. Guy accused of writing bad checks. I said, 'Could we get him to pay us in cash, you reckon?' But she was not amused."

"He's one of Powell's indigent clients, so I think the state will be footing the bill," Bill pointed out. "Besides, we're not supposed to think he's guilty."

"Uh-huh." Edith did not sound convinced. "Maybe you're not. I have to see that the bills get paid, and I balance the books for this firm. By the way, you got a message this morning. Do you feel up to taking it yet?"

"Depends. Is it Mr. Trowbridge with another crazy question?"

"No. It's somebody calling about that house ad you had me run in all those newspapers up north. He sounded interested." She held out a pink message slip. "Try not to sound too eager, though. In real estate deals it makes people suspicious."

"I'll keep that in mind," said Bill. He ambled off to his office to earn his keep.

He was pleased that a response to his ad had come so quickly, but he wasn't really surprised. It was a wonderful house. He had gone by to visit it at the first of last week, and it really was a period piece. (As were its inhabitants, he thought.) The white colonial house with Corinthian columns and a circular portico was in need of minor repairs—new shutters, perhaps, and a coat of paint—but its interior of hardwood floors and high-ceilinged rooms rich with carving was in perfect condition, lovingly cared for by its house-proud occupants. From the sweeping oak staircase in the front hall to the dormer rooms in the well-swept attic, the house was wonderful. Bill wished he could buy it himself, but the asking price of one million, five hundred thousand was well beyond his means. In fact, he would be hard-pressed to afford the paint for the shutters at his current income level.

Still, he supposed that someone living in the exorbitant urban sprawl between New York and Boston might consider one point five million a bargain price for six thousand square feet of historic house on three acres of oak-shaded lawns.

Bill decided that he wouldn't have any trouble conveying his enthusiasm for the property, which was just as well, because he thought that the conditions of sale verged on eccentric. They're little old ladies, he reminded himself. At their age, they're entitled to be a little strange. They were certainly charming when he visited them, though, dishing out slices of homemade chocolate cake with pecans and fussing over him as if he were a visiting prince. He wanted to sell their house for them as swiftly and profitably as possible so that they could retire to their suburban nursing home carefree and financially secure. The transaction would do wonders for his financial position as well. If it hadn't been for his bank's overdraft protection plan, Bill could easily have been another of his partner's bad-check cases.

Mentally ticking off the bills he could pay with his five percent commission, Bill dialed the phone number on the message slip.

Ten minutes later, in a considerably brighter mood, Bill placed another call, this one to Miss Flora Dabney at the Home for Confederate Women. By the time he heard her silvery voice on the other end of the line he was almost humming, his back problems and his parents' strife neatly banished from his thoughts. "Miss Flora? This is Bill MacPherson, your attorney, and I have good news."

"Has someone responded to your ad? So soon?"

"I just spoke to him and he's very interested in the house. His name is John Huff. He lives in Connecticut, but he'd like to acquire a house in Virginia."

Flora Dabney did not seem overly thrilled by the news. After a brief pause she said, "Did you tell Mr. Huff our terms, Bill?"

"Certified check? Yep. I explained that you wanted a quick sale, and that you didn't want the transaction tied up in bank-loan red tape. Mr. Huff said that there wouldn't be any problem about financing. I think he's loaded. He'd like to fly down and view the house. Would Wednesday afternoon suit you, Miss Flora? I promised I'd call back and let him know."

After a protracted silence, Flora Dabney said, "I suppose Wednesday would be all right. Will you be available that afternoon, Bill?"

"Yes, of course," said Bill, whose afternoons were usually spent doing crossword puzzles. "I thought I'd meet Mr. Huff at the airport and bring him out to the house. What time would you like us to arrive?"

There was another longish pause at the other end of the telephone. "Bill," Flora Dabney said at last, "we want you to show Mr. Huff the house. We'll leave the key in the mailbox for you."

"You want me—" Bill stared at the phone as if it had misquoted Flora Dabney.

"Yes. You show the house. We think that would be best. This house has been home to us for many years now, and naturally we feel a bit emotional about having to part with it, even though we have agreed that it's for the best. Still, I don't think any of us are up to the task of showing our beloved house to a stranger. Did he sound like a Northerner to you, Bill?"

"I guess so," said Bill, who hadn't given the matter any thought until now. "But don't you think you'd be in a better position to answer any questions he might have about the property? I've only been in the house once. What if I get lost?"

Flora Dabney's laugh was a silvery peal from a bygone belle. "Lost? Why, I just know that a clever young man like you couldn't possibly do a silly thing like that. And you probably know all those amazing things about wiring and plumbing that we are just mystified by. You'll do a splendid job of showing the Northern gentleman around. And don't you worry about having us old ladies underfoot. The eight of us will all go out to tea that afternoon, so we won't be in your way one little bit. Now phone Mr. Huff back and tell him that Wednesday will be perfectly fine."

"But what if he wants to buy the house? What if he wants to make an offer? Don't you want to meet him?"

"Why, no, Bill," said Flora Dabney. "It isn't necessary for us to meet the gentleman. We all trust your judgment."

At the sound of the dial tone Bill replaced the phone and began to paw through the papers on his desk in search of something to do. Amidst a stack of notes on Trowbridge questions, he found another pink memo with a message to himself in the angular handwriting of A. P. Hill. *Title Search!* the memo read.

Vaguely Bill remembered the conversation in which he had discussed the house sale with his busy law partner. Obviously she hadn't trusted him to remember her advice, which was just as well, because in fact the task had slipped his mind. Pocketing the square of paper, Bill strolled out into the reception area, where Edith was counting the paper clips.

"I have an important job for you," he announced in the hearty tones of one who hopes to be convincing.

"Go get your own hot dog," said Edith without looking up from her task.

"No, this is a legal assignment," Bill insisted. "I need you to go to the courthouse and look up the deed to a house. It's called a title search.

It's the sort of thing that legal secretaries do, while attorneys devote themselves to more technical matters."

"Okay," said Edith. "*You* count the paper clips."

"This will be time-consuming, but not difficult," said Bill, wisely choosing to ignore her comments. In fact, Bill had never done a real title search, although they had certainly studied the art in law school until he thought he would go mad from boredom. Carefully he explained the procedure to Edith: how to look in the deed books, how to follow the chain of ownership back from one property transaction to another. "This will probably be very simple," he assured her. "The house has belonged to the Confederate widows and daughters since the turn of the century. Just photocopy all the relevant pages and bring them back here, and I'll check over them."

Edith held out her hand. "I'll need dimes and quarters for the copy machine."

Bill fished out a handful of change from his pants pocket. There went lunch, he thought. After jotting down the salient points of the assignment on a yellow legal pad, Bill sent Edith off to the courthouse. Then he phoned John Huff with the good news: he could fly down on Wednesday and view the house.

◆　◆　◆

THE OFFICE OF JOHN HUFF was an elegant lair of oak paneling and green leather, but in his own mind, Nathan Kimball referred to it as the Roach Motel, and he secretly dreaded every visit he was forced to make to his client's inner sanctum. Kimball did not, of course, share these misgivings with the senior partners of Fremont, Shields, & Banks, because he was a very junior member of the law firm, and especially because John Huff was a wealthy and valued client. Mr. Huff did not, as far as Nathan Kimball could tell, spend his time evicting widows and orphans and tying village maidens to railroad tracks, but he looked as though he might. There was something of the nineteenth-century robber baron about Mr. Huff, and every time Nathan Kimball was obliged to visit him on legal business, he always found himself wishing that he had devoted his law practice to more mundane villains like car thieves. At least you knew where you stood with the small fry.

Huff, unconcerned with the tender feelings of his legal adviser, handed him a classified ad taped to a note card. "What do you think of that?" he demanded, dispensing as usual with preliminary civilities.

Kimball scanned the notice, a house-for-sale ad, with polite interest. There was a grainy photo of a structure reminiscent of Tara and a fulsome description of its amenities, which seemed to consist mostly of historic value, rather than practical accouterments such as air conditioning or master-bath Jacuzzis. Privately the attorney was wondering what he was expected to say. When inspiration failed, he murmured, "It's—er—quite large. And old. Old and large. Are you thinking of investing in real estate, Mr. Huff?"

Huff laughed. "I'm thinking of acquiring this place. The price isn't bad, but I think we might get them to come down a bit anyhow. I particularly like the location of the property."

Kimball consulted the ad again. The house was in Danville, Virginia. Where on earth was that? he wondered. On the beach? A suburb of Washington, perhaps? Next to an orphanage? "You know the area then, sir?" he ventured, suppressing a nervous giggle.

"Never been there in my life," Huff declared. "I suppose I will, though. Only a damn fool buys a piece of property sight unseen, and I am nobody's fool. I may want to close quickly though. Thought I'd better let you know. Make sure you keep Wednesday open."

"Er—this Wednesday?"

"Right. I'm going to fly down and take a look at the place. If it's suitable, we stay until we close. Shouldn't take but a day or so. The fellow I talked to down there doesn't sound any too shrewd, so there shouldn't be any difficulties. Still, I'll need you to go along. That's why I have lawyers. I expect you to look everything over, make sure it's all right. Mostly I want you there to look intimidating. Have you got a better suit, Kimball? And I hate that tie."

Nathan Kimball felt his face grow red as he fingered his birthday tie from Mother. He still felt that he was a few hundred yards behind in this conversation. "You want me to go with you to Virginia, sir?"

"Surely you grasped that," said Huff with a touch of acid in his voice. "Yes, Kimball, I want you to go to Virginia. Go home and pack your jammies, Kimball, and tell the firm that you're accompanying me on a business trip. We are going to purchase an historic house. Got it now?"

"But, sir, I know nothing about Virginia real estate law. Perhaps Mr. Shields—"

"You went to Yale, didn't you, Kimball? Surely you can contend with these rubes from Mayberry, whether you know their local customs or not. We're just going to buy a house, for God's sake. Think of it as a little vacation." John Huff bared his teeth in something resembling a grin.

"Yes, sir. Wednesday," said Nathan Kimball. But he certainly wouldn't think of it as a little vacation, he told himself. More like a white-collar skyjacking. For which he would have to go out and purchase a necktie. As he hurried out of the room, it occurred to him to ask Mr. Huff why on earth he wanted a house in Danville, Virginia. Somehow, though, the question wouldn't come out of his throat.

◆　◆　◆

A. P. HILL STILL FELT a little jittery when she entered the jail to confer with a client. As the steel door closed behind her, she always imagined walking into an escape in progress, and getting caught in the cross fire between guards and inmates. As usual, though, all was quiet within. Lonnie at the reception desk looked up from his paperwork long enough to wish her good morning; otherwise, the place seemed empty. She could hear the faint strains of the radio from beyond the door to the cells, and a stiff wave of disinfectant told her that it was cleaning time in the pens. She resolved to make her visit as brief as possible. Her client didn't require much counseling, anyway. It was a nothing case, almost certainly a plea bargain. That's why they had tossed it to her, the newest lawyer on the list.

"I'm here to see Tug Mosier again," she called out. "I'm his attorney." She was always careful to wear her most conservative blue suit, low-heeled pumps, and only the tiniest gold earrings for her trips to the county jail. Powell would never have admitted her nervousness to Bill or to any of her male colleagues; she hoped it didn't show. The best course seemed to be to do her job despite her fears and assume that sooner or later the anxiety would go away. A person could become used to anything, she reasoned; even to being locked in with dangerous felons.

"Tug Mosier, huh?" Lonnie whistled. "That's going to be some case."

"What do you mean? It's just worthless checks. Though I admit that he shouldn't have tried to post bail with another bad check. I may be able to get him off with time served."

"You mean you haven't heard yet? The finance company repossessed Tug Mosier's car yesterday because he made his car payment with one of his rubber checks."

"That's too bad, but it won't make any real difference to the case—"

"Don't bet on it, counselor. The finance company found Tug's girl-friend in the trunk. What was left of her."

A. P. Hill sat down on the waiting room bench without even remembering to dust it off first. She felt cold and out of breath at the same time. *Hot damn!* she thought, hugging her briefcase. *I've got my first murder case.*

◆   ◆   ◆

WHEN EDITH CREECH RETURNED from the courthouse, Bill was tidying his office. He had stacked his legal pads neatly on the corner of his desk. He had alphabetized the contents of his bookshelf. Now he was trying to dust the black-robed mascot Flea Bailey with his handkerchief.

"Hello! You're back!" said Bill. "Can you send dead groundhogs to the dry cleaner, do you think?"

Edith rolled her eyes. "They're gonna put you and Mr. Trowbridge in matching straitjackets. I got your paperwork here." She tossed a sheaf of photocopies onto Bill's just-dusted desk. "The house goes back to a Colonel Phillips in the late eighteen hundreds, and he left it to the Home for Confederate Women. It's all in there. Is that what you wanted?"

"Yes. Thanks! I already knew all that, but we had to have the documentation for the buyer. Just a formality. Oh, and while you were out, Powell called in to report her big news. Her bad-check guy just turned into a murder case."

"And A. P. Hill is defending him?"

"Right."

"Good," said Edith. "It's about time they stopped being soft on criminals around here. How are your cases going?"

"I've sent Mr. Trowbridge the kitten question, and I'm waiting for his next salvo. I show the Home for Confederate Women to the first prospective buyer on Wednesday." Bill laughed. "The buyer, Mr. Huff, wants me to meet him at the airport with a sign that says HUFF, so he can find me. I assured him that wasn't necessary, but he insisted. Remind me to make the sign between now and Wednesday."

"I'll do it," said Edith. "I print neater than you do. If he's picky enough to want a sign, he might as well have a good one."

"Thanks. Let's see: what else have I got done? Oh, I've filed Civil Action Number 90-CI-something-or-other in circuit court, which basically says that my dad will continue to make the house payments and pay the car insurance and so on at the old homeplace until we get the whole mess sorted out."

"Are you busy enough then, or do you want to run the newspaper ad advertising MacPherson and Hill for another two weeks? It's time to renew."

Bill thought about it. "Better run it," he advised. "We could use a few simple wills and speeding tickets to generate some revenue around here. Besides, Powell gets nervous if she has time to eat dinner."

Edith looked at her watch. "Well, I don't. If I don't feed my cat by six o'clock, he starts rooting in the houseplants. Pure spite, that's what it is. So if you don't need me for anything else . . ."

"No," said Bill. "I guess I could call it a night, too, since nobody seems to be clamoring for my services. Maybe I could stop in and see how Dad is doing in his new place."

"Isn't that a whattayacallit? An ex parte communication?"

"Not if we just talk about dinner . . . the Redskins . . . neutral topics. But—er—you don't have to mention this to my mother next time she comes in." Bill was the picture of abject misery. "Edith, have you ever been divorced?"

"It was a good while back, and it wasn't all that complicated. We didn't have anything worth squabbling over. We had an old trailer, a lot of debts, no kids, and not much love left to lose, so it went pretty quick. I won't be much help to you in figuring out your parents' situation."

"They're behaving so strangely. It's so hard to know how to fix it."

Edith Creech said gently, "Well, Bill, they didn't hire you to fix it."

◆　◆　◆

MARGARET MACPHERSON WAS NOT THINKING about her husband, Doug. She definitely was not. After five-thirty, the time when he would have been coming home from work, she had expended a considerable amount of energy ensuring that she would be much too occupied to remember his existence. She had watered the plants, vacuumed the spotless carpet, and reread the mail, even the bills and catalogues. In the background the television blared away for background noise, but she did not look at it. It was only a question of habits, she told herself; and one must be patient and give oneself time to change habits.

It would all take some getting used to. The rooms looked strange—with odds and ends of furniture missing from their accustomed places and none of Doug's usual clutter on the end tables. It was nice not to have to fix a complete meal every night, the meat and two vegetables that Doug insisted on. Now she could have a salad or a bowl of soup if she pleased, or just skip dinner altogether. Maybe she could lose a few pounds now that she was on her own. She looked at herself in the mirror above the fireplace. She might lighten her hair as well; it looked so mousy these days. Before, there hadn't seemed to be much reason to bother. It wasn't as if Doug ever noticed. She could have set it on fire and he wouldn't have remarked on it. Now, though, she thought she might try styling it. This was a time for trying things.

It was her turn now. The children were grown and launched into respectable careers. Her mind hovered over the word *respectable* in Elizabeth's case—all those cadavers—but at least she was married, and that's what counted. A stricken face stared back at her from the mirror as she listened to those sentiments. *At least she was married, and that's what counted.* Had she really thought such a thing? Her generation had been raised to believe that, and it was hard to outgrow that early indoctrination, even when you knew what a lie it was. That wasn't what counted at all. It mattered very much who you were, and what you did with your talents, because marriage these days was not a haven from the world. It was not the safety net; it was the tightrope.

Margaret MacPherson's gaze fell upon the family portrait, framed and hanging over the sofa. That could go in the attic, she thought. She could put another picture there reflecting the status of her new life—just as soon as she figured out what that was. She was brooding again. Time to get busy. Do the dishes, then, to keep occupied. She walked into the kitchen to tackle the day's dishes, only to find that she had already done them.

◆　◆　◆

On the way to Appomattox, the ghost of an army
Staggers a muddy road for a week or so
Through fights and weather, dwindling away each day.
—STEPHEN VINCENT BENÉT,
John Brown's Body, Book 8

DANVILLE—APRIL 9, 1865

COMPARED TO THE FAIR CITY of Richmond, Danville was
a piddling town, Gabriel Hawks reckoned. Perhaps the place was a mite
bewildered to be suddenly elevated to the capital of the Confederate
States of America and simultaneously flooded with refugees from the
former capital. Its citizens had scurried to find suitably grand accommo-
dations for the sudden rush of Confederate dignitaries who had taken
up residence in the little Dan River mill town now that Richmond was a

smoldering ruin. President Davis and two of his cabinet officers were guests in the home of Colonel W. T. Sutherlin, but there were too many refugees for Danville to accommodate, so some of the lesser folk were quartered in railroad cars switched off on a side track, where they subsisted on what commissary rations could be spared for them.

It seemed that most of the navy had fetched up in Danville. Gabriel had never seen so many captains, commanders, surgeons, and engineers, all milling around with nothing to do. They mostly congregated at the naval store set up by Paymaster Semple. There they'd pass the time sitting on bread barrels, tying fancy sailor's knots, and swapping sea yarns about past glories. But they were fish out of water. How could they still be in the war high and dry miles from the sea, their ships destroyed, their ports captured? But they simply had to wait it out, like the rest of Danville.

Tom Bridgeford had said that it was madness to have put the capital in Richmond to begin with, with all the vast territories of the Confederacy to choose from. Why not the grand port cities of New Orleans or Charleston? Why put the heart of your country a hundred and ten miles from the enemy's seat of government? One of the Richmond boys tried to explain to him that if the navy gunboats could have held off the Union fleet upriver, then the Allegheny Mountains would have forced any invading army down a hundred-mile corridor that would be made a death trap by the defending Army of Northern Virginia. The swamps and the forests ought to have swallowed them up, and indeed they did for three long years, but the trouble was the Union never ran out of soldiers. They just kept coming. No matter where you put the capital, they'd have just kept coming.

But Bridgeford wouldn't talk sense. It was all those damned Virginians' doing, he insisted. The Confederacy was top-heavy with them: Robert E. Lee, Thomas J. Jackson, A. P. Hill, J. E. B. Stuart—at least a hundred generals out of the four hundred altogether. *And* a raft of the government officials, all from the Old Dominion. President Davis was a Mississippian, but no doubt he was outvoted by all those Virginia gentlemen who demanded the honor of the seat of government for their precious Richmond—and common sense be damned. Well, look where it had got them, Bridgeford railed. After spending most of the war fending off the Federals from an endless succession of attacks on Richmond, they'd finally lost her and been forced to flee to this backwater place, whose only virtue, according to Bridgeford, was its proximity to the North Carolina line. Pride goeth before a fall.

Gabriel tried not to think about politics. Or losing the war. None of it made much sense to him, especially when you looked at the havoc that came of it all. But he thought that he might someday be old enough to tell the story of their retreat from Richmond for the comedy of errors that it was. He could laugh at it now *if* he hadn't been living it. "So there we was," he'd be telling his grand-younguns, "a-throwing pieces of that picket fence into the firebox on that locomotive and trying to get her a-going, and all the time we could hear them Yankees coming. Well, she finally built up a head of steam, and us sailors and a raft of the townsfolk clambered aboard, and off we chugged till we got to the first bit of a hill right outside the station near the riverbank, and she ground to a halt. That little locomotive wasn't equal to the task of hauling that great bulk of humanity any great distance, and there we sat, with a right smart view of the city of Richmond. We could see lines of Union cavalry and artillery snaking along toward State House Square, and we reckoned any minute they'd look up and see us, and that would be the end of us. But if the Lord wasn't on our side, then I reckon He sat that one out, 'cause they never paid us no mind, and besides, the bridges were all afire by then.

"By and by the steam engineer went running up to the admiral, and he must've told him about finding another locomotive hid away in the shops, because directly they went and hauled that engine out and hooked it on in front, and we were able to proceed at a crawl to the first decent woodpile. We lit out and grabbed the better fuel, and then we really fired up and got the hell out of Richmond."

The farther they got from the scene of destruction, the easier they breathed, and even now he could find things to laugh about on the run to Danville. It seemed like they couldn't go more than a mile without having to pick up a straggler—a stray colonel, even generals—left stranded by the recent turn of events. Then there were the railroad people. The admiral didn't appear overly amused by the sight of those conductors and engineers bustling out from their stations and trying to take over the operation of the train now that the navy had assembled it and got it going. He soon sent them off with a flea in their ears!

They reached Danville around midnight on April 4 and slept in the cars until sunup. Later, when news of the fighting farther north filtered into Danville, they learned what a narrow escape it had been. After turning Lee's flank at Five Forks, Sheridan's cavalry had attacked the Southside Railroad. They had torn up the rail at Burksville Junction just an hour and a half after Admiral Semmes's train had passed through there.

The orders to join General Lee in the field no longer stood. Admiral Semmes—now a brigadier general—organized the four hundred sailors left to his command into brigades. Hawks and Bridgeford were still serving under Captain Dunnington, who was now an army colonel.

"But we're still bottom of the heap," said Bridgeford. "Seems like the more it all changes, the more it stays the same for boys like us."

They were in the trenches on the outskirts of Danville now, defending the new capital from raiding parties, and waiting to see if the Union Army would turn its might on this last stronghold. The green of spring and the budding trees made a welcome change from the devastation of the blackened city they'd left behind, but a steady drizzle made the landscape drab, chilling them as they huddled in their mudholes. Sunshine would have made their watch more pleasant, but it would have done little for the scenery: no place in Virginia was really beautiful that May. The fields were untended stubble, with weeds and broken fences; everywhere the neglect of the war years showed in Danville's shabby appearance. Still, she was a luckier town than most of her sisters to the east.

"This is how I started out in this war," Gabriel Hawks replied. "Stuck in a mudhole with a rifle, waiting to get shot at. Things sure do stay mostly the same, don't they? You reckon they aim to pay us one of these days?"

Tom Bridgeford brushed the raindrops out of his face, making little rivulets in the streaks of dirt. "Hawks," he said, with an exasperated sigh, "what in Tophet does it matter? What salary do you draw now that you're an army private?"

"Eighteen dollars a month."

Bridgeford nodded. "Eighteen dollars a month Confederate scrip. That is correct. And how much is a barrel of flour going for in Danville these days?"

"If one could be had? A thousand dollars, maybe."

"And a turkey?"

Gabriel shrugged. "A hundred dollars easy. If they'd take your money."

"They'd a dern sight rather have gold. And it's more than fifty of our scrip dollars to buy a dollar in gold. So tell me, Hawks, what do you want your pay for? You tired of wiping your butt with corncobs, is that it?"

"I thought I might try to send some money home."

"Hawks, your kinfolk in the hills may be better off than we are, as long as there are deer in the woods and fish in the creek. But it does you credit to worry over them. I no longer have that burden."

Gabriel looked away. He knew that Bridgeford's parents and sister had passed away in Wilmington's yellow-fever epidemic in the fall of '62. Most likely that accounted for his bitterness about the state of the world. "I wish we could do something besides sit here," he said.

Bridgeford gave him a weary smile. "You could go home. Johnson has. Willets left last night. Every day a few more men sneak away when the officers' backs are turned. I don't believe Captain Dunnington has cottoned on to how easy it is to jump ship when you're in a ditch a hundred miles inland. How far is your farm from here? Fifty miles? Seventy? Why, you could—"

"Hold it! I saw something moving on the road!" Gabriel Hawks pointed to a shape just visible through the pines near the bend in the road. He shouldered his rifle. "Something's coming at us."

Bridgeford squinted into the distance. "It's wagons, looks like. And saddle horses alongside." He pushed Hawks's rifle barrel away from its aim. "Put that down. They're our people. I see a gray greatcoat in that first wagon. Don't suppose it serves a man well in this rain, though. Better than nothing, maybe."

Hawks shook his head. "I reckon they're another swarm of fugitives separated from their lines. Poor Danville! They might rather be invaded by the Federals than these starving Rebs—at least they'd bring their own provisions."

The somber procession tottered closer to the trenches. It was a sorry remnant of an army: walking skeletons shrunken inside their rags, wounded men barely able to stand and others on scarecrows of horses that looked as if they were walking their last mile. One soldier in oil-skins clambered out of his trench and waved down the battered wagon. "Where ye from?" he hollered at them. "What news?"

The rain pelted down, making creeks of the wagon tracks in the muddy road. From the wagon the gaunt faces stared back at them, showing no emotion but weariness. Finally the driver of the wagon, a chalk-faced soldier in the tatters of a uniform, looked down at the questioner with an expression that could have been grief—or disgust. "Guess y'all ain't heard," he said. "We abandoned the lines near a week ago. Lee surrendered his troops today at Appomattox Courthouse. Somebody said the rest was here, so we come on."

As the word spread from man to man, soldiers began to crawl out of the sodden trenches, congregating together on the road and questioning the ragged refugees, who seemed anxious to stagger on toward the town. "What must we do now?" they kept saying.

A newly appointed captain, formerly an officer on the *Virginia*, herded them back to their posts. "Our orders are to guard this town. The Federals may soon be coming after our president. We protect them until somebody tells us different." He looked around at the men under his command. "Hawks! Bridgeford! Escort these fugitives into town and see that their news is reported to Admiral—er, *General* Semmes. Tell him that we await further orders."

Still dazed from this thunderbolt of news, Gabriel felt himself stagger out of the ditch like a stunned ox. He felt Bridgeford's hand steadying him as he teetered on the edge of the embankment. "Is the war over, Tom?" he whispered, blinking away the wetness from his eyelashes.

"Not for us," muttered Bridgeford.

"I wish I was in the land of cotton."

—DANIEL D. EMMETT,
"Dixie"

CHAPTER

4

THE FLIGHT TO DANVILLE, Virginia, might have been relatively pleasant if it had started later in the day, and if they hadn't had to change planes in Pittsburgh. Still, it was too much to ask for a direct flight to such a tiny place, Kimball supposed. The possibility of arriving by turnip truck had crossed his mind. He had read all of *The New York Times* with more than customary thoroughness and had given up trying to find something worth reading in the in-flight magazine when the pilot made the landing announcement. Mr. Huff, who had slept fitfully for most of the journey, was still stretched out in the adjoining seat, dreaming with an unpleasant expression that suggested that he was playing the villain in his own nightmare. Kimball hated to awaken the sleeping dragon, but it had to be done. With some misgivings he nudged Mr. Huff gently and whispered, "We're coming into Danville, sir."

With reptilian alertness Huff opened his eyes and leaned over Kimball to peer out the window. "Call that an airport?" he growled.

Kimball longed to point out that Mr. Huff's own local airport, that of Westchester, New York, was about the size of a potting shed and contained tin-sheeted wooden baggage carousels that did not revolve, but he refrained from comment, rightly suspecting that the comparison would not be appreciated.

They gathered up their briefcases and made their way down the commuter plane's metal ladder onto the tarmac. A flight of steps took them inside the terminal to a small glassed waiting area, which was empty except for a blond young man, holding aloft a sign that read: I TOLD YOU SO. Nathan Kimball grinned, remembering Mr. Huff's insistence on being met with a welcoming sign. "I think that must be the sellers' attorney, Mr. MacPherson," he said, nodding toward the sign.

John Huff scowled at the placard. "Well, how was I to know?" he demanded of no one in particular. Then he seemed to make up his mind to be charming, because he thrust out his hand and assumed a brisk smile. "MacPherson! Good of you to meet us. When can we see the house?"

A flurry of introductions later, Bill replied, "We've been asked to wait until two o'clock to view the house, so as not to disturb the owners. They'll be out this afternoon, but I think that I can answer any questions you might have." He consulted his watch. "It's just on twelve now. Why don't I give you a quick tour of the city. It's a rather historic place, you know. And then we can get some lunch at Ashley's Buffet."

"Yes, I'm rather interested in history," said John Huff. "I've heard of Danville."

"Everybody has, thanks to Johnny Cash," said Bill. "I can show you where the train wreck was, though of course it's all built over now. There is a historical marker."

Huff stared at him. "Did you say *train* wreck?"

"Yes. The wreck of the old 97. It's a folk song. Johnny Cash recorded it a good while back. Isn't that how you heard of Danville?" Bill hummed a few bars of the song. " 'It's a mighty rough road from Lynchburg to Danville, And a line on a three-mile grade.' That's us."

Nathan Kimball fought back giggles as he tried to picture Mr. Huff as a fan of country music while that austere gentleman himself seemed to be choking on unspoken comments. Their native guide, happily oblivious to the visitors' reactions, prattled on about Dan River textiles and pit-cooked barbecue. "And we do have one local celebrity. Have you ever heard of Wendell Scott?"

For the first time Huff looked interested. "General Winfield Scott of the Mexican War? I didn't know he—"

"No, sir, not him. Wendell Scott, the stock car racer. Richard Pryor played him in a movie called *Greased Lightning*. He was from right around here, but I think they shot the film somewhere else. They usually do."

"We'd very much like to see the city," said John Huff in tones of strangled politeness.

"Of course, if you're thinking of moving here, you probably have a lot of practical questions about the area," said Bill. "What sort of business are you in, sir?"

"I am an investor, but American history is something of an avocation for me. I understand this house we'll be looking at has some historic significance."

"Yes sir. It dates back to the 1840s, and as you know, it has been used as the Home for Confederate Women since the turn of the century."

"May I know to whom it belonged before that time?" asked Mr. Huff. "Was it by any chance a Colonel W. T. Sutherlin?"

"No," said Bill, looking surprised. "According to the information on the deed, the house was owned by a Mr. Phillips."

John Huff smiled. "Even better!" he declared, and strode off toward the parking lot, leaving the two attorneys scrambling after him to wonder why he had suddenly seemed so pleased.

◆   ◆   ◆

A. P. HILL HAD NEVER LOOKED FORWARD to a date with anything like the eagerness with which she anticipated her twenty-minute interview with Tug Mosier. She felt a shiver of excitement at the prospect of defending someone against the most serious of charges: first-degree homicide.

She would have to keep reminding her mother that Tug Mosier was technically innocent until a jury said otherwise, because the word from southwest Virginia was that the Hill family did not think much of the idea of their little Amy associating with the likes of the defendant. In her excitement over her first major case, Powell had phoned home with the news, only to learn that murder cases did not fall under the heading of a godsend in her parents' estimation. There was even talk of having Cousin Stinky look into the matter, which Powell Hill definitely did not want, because Stinky knew so many good old boys in legal circles that he could probably get her taken off the case ("in the best interests of the accused") in a New York minute.

The powers-that-be would be delighted to replace her with a Silverback, and they'd probably think they were doing Tug Mosier a favor. In fact, she had already had a similar conversation with the courthouse Silverback, and he had allowed her to keep the case, but his misgivings in the matter were evident. He had advised Powell Hill to plea-bargain, and to avoid a trial at all costs. That wasn't a decision she felt she could make yet, but one thing was certain: she had better do a good job on this case. Her immediate future was riding on it.

A. P. Hill's client was hunched in a wooden chair, awaiting their conference without apparent interest. She looked at him appraisingly, trying to see Tug Mosier as a jury would. He would not do, she decided. She would have to see about getting Tug some presentable clothing before his court appearance; the jury and the press (not to mention her family) really would freak if they could see him in his present unshaven glory. He looked like the sergeant-at-arms for a biker gang. His shoulder-length brown hair seemed to have been styled with Quaker State, and a blue dragon tattoo peeped out from under the sleeve of his undershirt on a flabby arm the color of a fish belly. There wasn't much she could do about the close-set piggy eyes and his habitual truculent scowl, but a suit and a haircut might soften the effect. She wondered how to bring up the topic without offending him, and decided to start their conversation with a less delicate subject.

"How's it going, Tug?" she asked. "Are you getting enough to eat?"

He shrugged. "Not too hungry anyhow. Not with all this hanging over me."

"The charges are very serious. The prosecution is saying that you killed Misti Lynn Hale and put her in the trunk, intending to take the body off somewhere and bury it. They say that if you hadn't been put in jail on the bad-check charge, you'd have ditched the evidence, and maybe they wouldn't have caught you. You need to tell me your side of the story so that we can begin to build a defense."

Tug Mosier put his head in his hands. "You won't believe me."

"It's my job to believe you. It's the jury you have to worry about."

"Okay, I'll tell you. What the hell. You know I've been laid off from my welding job; that's why I had trouble paying the bills. And those collection-agency people just kept calling and calling and nagging us about it and making Misti cry, so I wrote them dud checks just to get a little peace and quiet. Figured they'd leave us alone—at least till they bounced."

"I can certainly see the temptation," A. P. Hill agreed.

"I thought it would make me feel better, but I was still miserable, 'cause I knew it was just postponing the flak. So I got tanked up to try to put it out of my mind."

His attorney raised her eyebrows. "Define tanked up."

"I did some coke and some shine. I was with some old boys I been knowing for a long time, and by the end of the evening we were purt near blasted."

Defendent used cocaine and bootleg liquor and admits to a state of complete intoxication, A. P. Hill wrote on her yellow legal pad. She looked up and nodded for her client to continue.

"So I don't remember too awful much about that night at all. I know I went home. The next thing I knew, I was sort of coming out of it—somewhere between waking up and walking out of a fog—and there was Misti Lynn, laying on the floor, not moving."

"Was she dead? Could you see any injuries?"

Tug Mosier frowned with the effort of remembering. "She wasn't moving. I couldn't see no blood."

"All right." There would have been no blood. Misti Lynn Hale had been strangled. "Was there anyone else present?"

Tug Mosier rubbed his scalp as if he were trying to massage his brain cells. He squinted at the bare green wall beyond the table. "That's the funny thing," he said at last. "Seems like I sorta remember somebody going home with me. Helping me, like. 'Cause I wasn't in no shape to do much walking on my own. But when I came to and saw my Misti on the kitchen floor, there wasn't nobody around."

"So what did you do once you realized that she was dead? Did you call anybody?"

Tug Mosier looked shocked at his attorney's naïveté. She probably would find a dead body on her floor and call somebody about it, his expression seemed to say. "No," he said wearily. "I didn't call nobody. I've had a run-in or two with the cops before, and I didn't think I'd have too much luck making them believe in my innocence."

"What did you do, then?"

"I picked up Misti Lynn and I put her in the trunk of my car. I couldn't just leave her laying there. I don't know what I was fixing to do with her. Maybe take her to the hospital, or just leave her somewhere. I don't know. I kind of blacked out again. We had some pills in the medicine cabinet, and I think I took a couple of them. Anyhow, next thing I knew, the cops were banging on the door with their warrant about those damn checks, and it just plain slipped my mind about her being in the trunk."

"Why didn't you tell me about her when I first talked to you about the check charge?"

He shrugged. "Figured maybe they wouldn't find her. I guess I was hoping I dreamed it."

Powell Hill stared at her client. There really were people in the world who could forget about having a woman's corpse in the trunk of their car. Or if they dimly remembered, they might ignore it, hoping that it would go away. His story rang true. It wasn't much help with his defense, though. As far as she could tell, not even he knew if he had killed her or not.

◆　◆　◆

FLORA DABNEY LOOKED at her watch. It was time to start getting ready to go. At least it was time to tell Anna Douglas to start getting ready, because she always took twice as long as anybody else. It wasn't really vanity on Anna's part, Flora decided; it was just that Anna was a methodical person, and the good Lord had only given her first gear, so there was no use in trying to speed her up. Anna had lived in the Home for twenty years now and her housemates hadn't found anything yet that could make her hurry. After a long spell of getting upset and angry over Anna's slowness, Flora and the others had learned to give her an extra hour's notice whenever they wanted her to do anything. It saved worry all the way around.

They had all been together for such a long time that they were like family now. At eighty-three, Flora had outlived her own sister by a dozen years, but they hadn't been close since childhood. Flora married late, staying home to care for her invalid father, while her pretty younger sister had married a man from Alabama and moved far away. Finally their lives did not touch at any point. Common circumstances and decades of living together had made these seven women more her sisters than blood ties ever could. Flora felt responsible for all of them, even the exasperating Julia Hotchkiss, who looked like a bird but could eat more than a mule. They needed someone who could take care of them, and after time's winnowing, Flora was left as the strongest in body and mind; so it fell to her to look after the others. Dolly Smith was her closest friend and she was certainly no fool, but arthritis had nearly crippled her, weakening her fighting spirit. She needed better health care than they could afford.

The others needed tending as well. Mary Pendleton was too trusting for her own good, and Ellen Morrison would rather let people walk all over her than risk offending them. Lydia had lost interest in everything in the world except her precious family tree, and Jenny Wade Allan was all but an invalid. Without Flora they would be at the mercy of any sharpster or bureaucrat who came down the pike.

Until recent years there had been other people that they could rely on: Mr. Bowers, their attorney, who was overseer of the Home for Confederate Women trust; a housekeeper-manager who supervised the running of the property; and a couple of daily maids who saw to the cooking and the cleaning. But Mr. Bowers had died, and inflation meant that prices kept going up while their income stayed about the same. Then the housekeeper resigned, so now there was only one aging maid to look after them. She cooked a little and cleaned every now and then, but it wasn't enough. The house had begun to take on a general air of neglect and they were powerless to stop its decline. The limited income from the trust would not stretch to more than basic mainte-nance, at least not if they wanted to keep purchasing food. A broken furnace or a leaky roof would spell disaster for the eight remaining residents of the Home. Really they were running out of choices, just as they had run out of people to help them. Flora felt that it was up to her to take care of the others.

She looked around the spacious, sunny bedroom that had been her lair for more than twenty years. The wallpaper was faded and the ceiling a road map of plaster cracks, but still she loved it. It was familiar and comfortable, and still bore traces of a bygone elegance—like a grande dame who had fallen on hard times. The best bits of the Dabney family furniture were displayed about her, and on a mahogany chest sat her mother's tea service of Mexican silver. Flora wished that she could continue to live there, but modern times being what they were, that wish was a pipe dream.

She looked at her reflection in the mirror. Her white hair was carefully arranged in wings at the sides of her head, caught up in a knot at the nape of her neck. The lavender dress was a little old, perhaps, but then who noticed style in an old lady, and what did she care for the opinion of those young pups who ran the world these days? She opened the dresser drawer and took out her white gloves. It was time to make themselves scarce. Lydia could take the bus to the courthouse, and she would ask Reba to drive the rest of them to the mall for a few hours.

There was a tap at the door, and Mary Lee Pendleton peeped in. "Are you ready, Flora? I was hoping that we could have lunch at the cafeteria while we were out there."

"All right, Mary. It's an extravagance, but I suppose we could afford it now. We should go soon. I told Mr. MacPherson to bring them by about two."

"Being run out of our home by Yankees," sighed Mary. "Well, that's nothing new."

◆　◆　◆

IN HIS CHROME-AND-GLASS OFFICE on the twelfth floor of the bank building, Doug MacPherson was contemplating his lunch: a turd of tuna salad on wilted lettuce, enthroned in a Styrofoam tray—and a cellophane packet containing an assortment of stress vitamins. A few weeks ago he would have felt deprived for having to eat such meager fare, but now the gastronomic austerity made him feel young and invigorated. He pictured his waistline trimmer after a few weeks of such noontime abstinence, and he fancied that he could feel his blood pressure and his cholesterol level creeping steadily down to acceptable levels. A return of his thinning hair was perhaps too much to expect from raw vegetables and vitamins, but at least the attrition might be slowed by this new attention to nutrition. Anything so nonfilling and unappetizing ought to be able to work miracles, he told himself, but he banished this thought as unworthy and socially incorrect. Caroline would not approve of such an attitude. It was she who had ordered this lunch for him, and he was flattered that she should be so concerned with his health. Similar suggestions about his choice of diet had come regularly over the years from his wife, Margaret, but those he had dismissed as nagging, merely the food fads of a foolish woman. From Caroline, they were expressions of her tender concern, and as he gulped down his vitamin tablet, he raised his mineral water in a silent toast to her.

Life was no longer boring. Of course the children were outraged and embarrassed, and Margaret was behaving as if he had taken to peeing on lampposts, but he was rather enjoying all the fuss. It made him feel young again. He was someone to whom adventures might still occur, not the stagnated man of middle years who'd had stuffed peppers for dinner every Monday night since the Carter administration. The exhilaration of this new freedom was worth any amount of family strife, he thought. It was his life, wasn't it? And he wasn't going to live forever, so he might as well make the most of things while he still had his health. Besides, he'd worked very hard for a great many years to provide for those ungrateful offspring of his, and he had given Margaret a very comfortable home indeed. Who were they to criticize him?

Of course the apartment he now lived in was a squalid nuisance, compared with his old residence, but it was only a minor annoyance, and a very temporary one at that. As soon as the divorce was settled, he would move into a place more in keeping with his current lifestyle. And surely by then he wouldn't have to do all those irritating domestic chores for himself. Cooking was a great bother after a hard day's work; usually he decided that he couldn't face it and he ate out. And he was certainly tired of having to use the cramped and musty laundry room in the basement of the apartment building every time he ran out of clean underwear. A few times he had given in and simply bought a new package at J.C. Penney's, but that was *not* cost-effective.

All in all, he was doing just fine without Margaret. He felt alive again. But hungry. Still hungry. He looked down at the empty Styrofoam tray. Even the lettuce was gone. With a furtive glance at the closed door of his office, Doug MacPherson began to rummage in his desk for the breath mints.

◆   ◆   ◆

BILL MACPHERSON MIGHT HAVE enjoyed a quiet lunch with Nathan Kimball. They could have talked about their respective law practices and swapped law-school yarns, but the presence of the glacial Mr. Huff made such small talk impossible. Apparently he was too wealthy to bother to be pleasant.

Bill soon realized that John Huff was not interested in the particulars of life in the charming city of Danville, and he was at a loss to think of some other topic that might interest his guests. Huff seemed equally lukewarm on the subject of area golf courses, recreational lakes, and local cultural events. Kimball made a few fitful attempts to keep the conversation going, but he didn't seem to know what Mr. Huff was interested in, either. In the end, they ate their chicken and dumplings in a strained silence, punctuated by innocuous remarks about the weather. Bill found that he was glancing at his watch approximately every ninety seconds.

Finally the minute hand crawled up to twelve, and he was able to down the last of his iced tea and announce with forced heartiness, "If you're sure you wouldn't like something else to eat, we can drive out and see the house now."

He took the expressway to the exit for the old part of the city, the kernel of graceful houses and tree-lined boulevards that lay within the layers of interstates and neon strips encircling the original settlement. John Huff sat silently in the front passenger seat, observing their progress without apparent emotion, but Nathan Kimball peered out the window, exclaiming over various splendid examples of neoclassical architecture.

"And these date from before the Civil War?" he asked.

"A lot of them, I guess," said Bill, whose interest in architecture had stopped with his tree house at the age of nine.

"But I thought General Sherman burned all the mansions in the South."

"I believe he only did that from Atlanta to Savannah," said Bill diffidently. "You know, Georgia. I expect my law partner A. P. Hill would know. She's descended from the general."

"Which general?" asked Kimball.

"Oh, never mind," murmured Bill. "Here's the house. It's quite large, as you can see. It could stand a coat of paint, but the Orkin man assures us that it's free of termites; the woodwork is perfectly sound. And these oak trees are all healthy, too. They're over a hundred years old as well."

"Very nice," grunted Huff.

"It looks like Tara!" said Nathan Kimball admiringly.

Bill concluded from this remark that Kimball either hadn't seen the movie or hadn't been paying attention when he did, because in fact the Home for Confederate Women was considerably grander than the O'Hara's North Georgia farmstead as depicted in *Gone With the Wind*. This Virginia mansion was a three-story white frame building built in an L-shape with an arched carriageway on one side, topped by a glassed-in sun porch. The front of the building was adorned with a circular portico supported by four Corinthian columns. Bill hoped that the subject of heating bills wouldn't come up during the showing of the house.

He parked the car on the paved loop behind the carriageway and led the way up the flagstone path to the front door. "They've left the key in the mailbox for us," he said, stopping to retrieve it. "It's a very safe neighborhood. I think the ladies were shy about showing their home to strangers. And of course they didn't want you to feel *pressured*," he said to John Huff.

"I never feel pressured," Huff replied.

Bill unlocked the door and escorted the visitors into an oak-paneled hallway that extended the length of the house. To their right was a flight of stairs with an elaborately carved banister and newel post. The carpet was threadbare and the dusty light fixture did not sufficiently illuminate the hall, but traces of the home's former splendor were still evident in the workmanship and the materials used. "There are three stories to the house," Bill told them, stealing a glance at an index card he'd concealed in the pocket of his blazer. "And a full basement. The third floor has been sealed off for many years, as the number of residents diminished. All in all, though, there are ten bedrooms in the house, and"—another peek at his notes—"eight baths. One on the first floor; the rest are upstairs. The main parlor is to your left. The ornamental plasterwork is original."

John Huff inspected every room in the house with meticulous care while the two attorneys trailed after him, making what they hoped were intelligent remarks. He examined all three floors, paying particular attention to the shelves of books in the first-floor library. Bill had never heard of most of the titles, but the books were certainly old, many of them were leather bound, and they were probably valuable.

"I would expect these to be included in the sale of the house," said Huff.

"I'll mention that to my clients," Bill stammered.

"Is there an attic?"

"I think so," said Bill. "Would you like to see it?" He was trying to remember how to get there.

"Perhaps later," said Huff. "When we looked in the basement, I noticed that there were some trunks and boxes. What about them?"

"I'll ask. Do you want that stack of *National Geographic*s down there, too?"

"Everything. Also, do you have any information as to what role this house played in the Civil War?"

"Nothing much," said Bill, who didn't have to consult his notes for that. He considered it the weakest link in his sales pitch. "I mean, Robert E. Lee didn't sleep here or anything. Of course, Danville was the last capital of the Confederacy, for about ten days in 1865 when nobody cared anymore. You know that song, 'The Night They Drove Old Dixie Down'? When Joan Baez sings that line about being on the Danville train, that's what she's talking about."

"Country music seems to have been a vast educational resource for you," said Huff. "I believe we were discussing this house during that time."

"Oh, right. Well, as I said, it was here then, but it wasn't used for government business. I think that the Phillips family played host to some minor Confederate officials. People named—" He peeked at his card. "Miss Dabney wrote this out for me in case you turned out to be a history buff. Umm . . . here it is. A Mr. Micajah Clark, a Mr. Semple, and the postmaster general, a Mr. Reagan. Wonder if he's any relation?"

"I think not," said Huff, looking singularly unamused. Bill got the impression, though, that there had been a flash of recognition in his cold eyes at the recital of that list of names.

They finished their tour in the antiquated kitchen, but John Huff did not seem dismayed by the lack of modern appliances or the faded linoleum and drab green walls. "It's a big room," Bill said lamely. "It has possibilities."

"So does garbage," muttered Nathan Kimball to himself.

"I've seen enough," John Huff announced. "I'll be staying in town a few days. Perhaps you could recommend a hotel?"

"Sure," said Bill. "There's the Stratford Inn, the Best Western on Highway 58—"

"Never mind. We'll look in the phone book. As I was saying, Kimball and I will be staying a few days. If at the end of that time we find that everything checks out—the appraisal, the survey, and so on—then I'll make your clients an offer for the house."

"Did I mention their terms?" asked Bill, waiting for the deal to come crashing down as he spoke. "I'm afraid they're rather eccentric about business matters. They don't seem to trust banks. It's probably the result of having lived through the Depression, don't you think? Anyhow, they don't want to be bothered with financing."

"I understand. If the details all check out, I'll be prepared to offer them a cashier's check for the full amount. I will, of course, expect a discount for cash."

"I'll tell them," Bill promised. "I expect you'll be meeting them at closing, so if there's anything else you'd like to know about the house, perhaps you can ask them then."

John Huff nodded. "Well, there is one thing. Do you happen to know if there are any secret passages in the house?"

◆ ◆ ◆

One day he is there and smiling.
The next he is gone as if he had taken fernseed
And walked invisible so through the Union lines.
You will not find that smile in a Northern prison
Though you seek from now till Doomsday.

—STEPHEN VINCENT BENÉT,
John Brown's Body, Book 8

WASHINGTON, GEORGIA—MAY 5, 1865

GABRIEL HAWKS WAS now a lieutenant in the army, but the honor of the field promotion paled somewhat when he considered how little competition remained for a position in the ranks of Confederate officers. After Lee surrendered the Army of Northern Virginia at Appomattox Courthouse on Palm Sunday, President Davis and the Confederate government had left Danville by train and proceeded to

Greensboro, North Carolina, to confer with General Joseph E. Johnston and General P. G. Beauregard about the fate of the Cause.

Most of the lower ranks felt no need to wait for further advice about
the outcome of the war. They were deserting from the train at every
station, leaving their posts and their comrades, and slipping away to
lose themselves in the tide of fugitives heading for home. Gabriel
couldn't say that he blamed them. How could anyone doubt that the
war was lost in the face of the evidence of his own eyes? One of the
soldiers who had been in the cabinet car was telling it all over about
how he saw the secretary of the navy and the adjutant general passing a
tin cup of coffee back and forth, for want of utensils, while the secretary
of state himself was dipping his dinner out of a haversack of hard-
boiled eggs. The soldier said they bore it all cheerfully, even joking
about these sorry circumstances—and perhaps that was the worst sign
of all. Surely the end was near.

Gabriel Hawks might have run, too. He was thinking about it as the
train headed westward into Piedmont, North Carolina. He could follow
the New River north and be back in Giles County before June. But then
the navy's paymaster James Semple had made him a lieutenant, and he
felt he ought to set an example for the rest. Bridgeford laughed at him,
of course, but then they made him a lieutenant, too, so there they were,
in ragged, ill-fitting uniforms scrounged from somewhere by Mr. Semple. They hoped they wore deserters' coats, not the leavings of dead
men. Still, they were officers.

"The rise in pay delights me," Bridgeford drawled. "Now it will only
take us three months to save up our wages for a pound of butter."

"That is, if they pay us at all."

"True, Hawks. And well noted. But, hell, we may as well stick it out a
while," Bridgeford said, laughing. "Maybe Johnston can whip Sherman
in Carolina. Maybe the damned Texans will march across the Missis-
sippi and win the war for us yet. Then we'll be fixed for life."

"You think they will?" Hawks had asked him, feeling a shiver of
hope.

"No," said Bridgeford. "But look out there." He pointed to the rolling vista of cornstalks, brown and broken behind crumbling fences. "It's
the same everywhere, Hawks."

It *was* the same everywhere. Hawks knew that. The Yankees' General
Sheridan had laid waste to most of Virginia. The Richmond paper had

quoted a message that Sheridan sent to Lincoln: "If a crow were to fly across the Shenandoah Valley, he would have to take his rations with him."

"And I've no family left," Bridgeford went on. "I've grown accustomed to being hungry. What does it matter if we go or stay?"

So they had stayed, and when the train rumbled into Greensboro with only two hundred and fifty men aboard, Hawks and Bridgeford were still among that number. Some of the men joked that they'd just keep on riding the train to Mexico; they had been traveling on it for more than a week already. After a few days' wait in Greensboro, the train ride began again; but this time the government officials were not aboard.

Word had it that Joe Johnston was going to surrender his army, too. They'd all heard reports of what he'd told the government officials. One of the orderlies could tell it off by heart: " 'I shall expect to retain no man beyond the by-road or cow-path that leads to his home. My small force is melting away like snow before the sun, and I am hopeless of recruiting it.' " The Confederacy had fallen with Robert E. Lee; only the politicians seemed ignorant of that fact. It was at last decided that Johnston would surrender his army, but political leaders would continue to retreat, perhaps to continue the fighting farther south, or failing that, to set up a government in exile in Mexico or in Europe.

On April 16 the presidential party disbanded to go their separate ways, some on horseback, some in wagons and ambulances, all heading south, and all with a few soldiers for escort. There was word that Stoneman's cavalry was combing the area in search of Jefferson Davis, and the officials believed that a scattering of several groups of fugitives would increase the president's chances of getting away. The train continued on as before, as an added decoy for the Union pursuers, now escorted by a mounted guard of Admiral Semmes's forces to fend off the enemy cavalry. Their protection was more than a decoy for the opposition. The train in itself was well worth defending, for in one of its cars was the contents of the Confederate treasury: silver coin and gold bullion transported from Richmond with the evacuation of the government.

The tattered caravans wended their way south, following muddy roads past blackened chimneys and stubbled fields that would mean more hunger in the months to come. They stopped in Charlotte, North

Carolina, for a week-long stay, where news of Lincoln's assassination reached President Davis, but there was no rejoicing over the passing of their old adversary. He was thought a fair man, and one whose death boded only ill for the Southern people. Word of Johnston's surrender was telegraphed to the anxious cabinet, and then a message from Johnston that the Union had denied Sherman permission to offer lenient terms of surrender. The flight was on again.

From Charlotte, North Carolina, the parties proceeded to Yorkville, South Carolina, with an escort of more than two hundred cavalry, troops escaping from Johnston's surrender. They scouted the area for enemy troops and escorted the cabinet to the Greenville Railroad, on which they traveled to Cokesville. The Union forces were in hot pursuit; Davis was roused in the middle of the night to flee from enemy troops just ten miles from the town. Despite the fugitive nature of the government's journey, its progress was never secret. The opposing forces always knew where they were going, and at each stop, the townspeople met them with cheering crowds and offers of hospitality. But the goodwill of the citizens would not protect them from the wrath of the victors; a capture would mean prison or the gallows.

They fled to Abbeville, arriving there on the second of May, but they didn't stay long. While the Confederate cabinet was holding its last meeting at the home of Colonel Armistead Burt, the train pulled into the depot, still guarded by Semmes's forces, and a change in personnel was made. George Trenholm, the secretary of the treasury, had been left ill near the Catawba River, and now the president appointed Postmaster John H. Reagan acting treasurer of the Confederacy. Reagan took charge of the train and ordered the cavalry to proceed to Washington, Georgia, forty-five miles to the south. When it arrived, he relinquished the office of treasurer to Captain Micajah Clark, formerly chief clerk of Jefferson Davis's executive office. That transfer of authority was the last official signature affixed by the president to any document.

Hawks and Bridgeford knew nothing of these transactions of power. They accompanied the train on its southward procession, obeying whatever orders were given. They knew, though, that the train could not be guarded safely much longer. And more men were anxious to leave the service of the dying nation. How foolish it would be to die in an eleventh-hour battle for a country that no longer existed.

At Washington, Georgia, General Breckinridge demanded that the treasurer pay his troops out of the remaining funds. The soldiers' paper money was worthless, and they would need money to make their way home, and so the quartermasters made out their payrolls and paid each man about twenty-six dollars in coin, enough perhaps to see them safely through.

Since the train was no longer a safe means of transportation, the forces disbanded one last time. Stephen Mallory, secretary of the navy, remained in Washington, Georgia, and Mr. Benjamin of the cabinet faded away before Jefferson Davis was captured at Irwinsville on May 10. The others were heading for Florida, hoping to outrun and outlast their pursuers.

Hawks and Bridgeford were among the small band of ex-navy men who accompanied Paymaster James A. Semple on the final leg of the journey to nowhere in particular. In their charge were a couple of wagons, containing the remnants of the navy's supplies and rations. The paymaster was a legend in the military for the resourcefulness of his scrounging. In Danville, he was even lending supplies to some of the army personnel. Hawkes wondered if he'd ever taste real coffee again. The concoction of mashed peanuts that they were drinking went by the name of coffee, but the taste wouldn't fool a lap baby. The stuff was hot, and that was about all you could say for it. The food alone would make a man desert, never mind the hopelessness of a lost war. Going home meant meat without maggots, fresh eggs and vegetables, and maybe a dash of salt again.

"We have little enough to show for serving our country," said Bridgeford as they rode along beside the wagon. His horse was a bag of bones covered with skin; its head drooped with exhaustion under the weight of its rider. "I have a few silver coins and a Confederate penny given to me by Admiral Semmes, a ragged coat, some scars, and the rank of lieutenant in a defeated army. It isn't much of a start for my career as a civilian."

"It makes me no never mind," said Hawks. "I was a farmer before; reckon I will be again. All I lost was time."

"Doesn't it bother you any that you gave four years of your life for nothing?"

"Wish we coulda won," shrugged Hawks. "But there's a lot gave more than I did. General Jackson did. The boys I joined up with—most of them won't be going back at all."

Tom Bridgeford slowed his horse to let the wagon go ahead of them. "That's war for you. Nobody wins but the politicians. Why, I bet as soon as the ink is dry on the peace treaties, the career officers will be worming their way back into the Union Army, and the politicians will be trying to get appointed to offices under whatever government is running things. It's the rest of us who'll be out of luck, broke in health and nothing to show for it."

"They made us officers," Hawks pointed out. "My folks will be mighty proud of that."

"Well, my folks are dead," said Bridgeford. "In an epidemic that happened thanks to this war, and the way I see it, the noble Confederacy still owes me a considerable debt of gratitude."

Gabriel Hawks smiled at his friend. "You want them to make you a general, Tom?"

Bridgeford eased his horse close to Hawks's plug mare. Looking about him to see that no one was watching, he leaned over and whispered, "Do you know what's in that middle wagon, Gabriel Hawks?"

The bantam farmer from the Blue Ridge shook his head. "Blankets, maybe. Hardtack?"

"Think again. I looked this morning before we started rolling. The whole Confederate treasury went with us on the train when we left Danville. And when the group disbanded in Little Washington, they paid the soldiers, and then they divided up the rest of the money. Mr. Semple carried off about eighty bars of gold bullion in that wagon."

Hawks paled and glanced at the covered wagon. It was battered and muddy; it didn't look like a rolling treasure chest. "But that gold is government money, Tom."

"What government? Lee surrendered, and those men we've been escorting for a month are headed for the ends of the earth. You want to turn it over to the Yankee government so maybe they can pay their soldiers to come burn some more of our farms?"

"I'm no thief," said Hawks. They rode on in silence for a couple of minutes while he mulled it over. "I can't think of anybody that ought to have that money, though." Bridgeford said nothing. "Still, I wouldn't kill nobody for it," said Hawks.

"Reckon I wouldn't either," said Bridgeford, cantering ahead.

They didn't say any more about it that day. They just kept heading southeast, trying to outrun the enemy and avoid the bands of raiders who prowled the undefended roads. When DeBruhl was shot by bush-whackers and Glover's cough got so bad he couldn't sit up anymore, there were only six of them. Doyle, the dark-eyed youth from Alabama, slipped away to go home, and Semple took the others to go scouting and foraging, leaving his two lieutenants in a clump of woods to guard the wagons. At dusk they hadn't returned, so Hawks and Bridgeford took turns standing guard all night. They dared not risk a campfire.

When the sky turned clabbered with daylight, Hawks, who hadn't been asleep, got up and put his ragged blanket back in the wagon. "You there, Tom?" he called softly.

From the shadows of the pines, Bridgeford emerged, his rifle balanced in the crook of his arm. Even the crickets were quiet. He turned to look out at the white ribbon of road, still and silent in the graying light. "They're not coming back," he said.

Hawks turned to look at the wagon. He licked his lips and shivered a little from the night air. "They should have been here by now."

"I guess we ought to move on out of here before whoever got them finds us," said Bridgeford. He looked for a long time at the tarp-covered wagon they had guarded through the night. "I don't think it would be wise to take that along," he said at last. "If Mr. Semple does come back, he'd hunt us down for sure if we made off with the wagon, and even if he didn't catch us, we'd attract too much attention. I don't have a mind to fight it out with bushwhackers along these roads, even for a ton of gold."

Hawks nodded. "It's more money than we'd need in a lifetime, and it would seem foolish to die after we done lived through the war."

Bridgeford began to saddle his horse. "I haven't seen Semple so much as look at the gold since we left Little Washington. I don't reckon he'd miss half a dozen bars. At least, not in time to catch us."

He burrowed in under the tarp and lifted out a brick of Confederate gold, dull in the dawn grayness. "It's heavy, right enough," he said, handing it to Hawks. "I make it twenty pounds. Thirty, perhaps. We could put them in our haversacks, if we got rid of some provisions. I think my horse could bear the weight of three of them if I let him take his time on the journey."

"Three of them would be a deal of money," said Hawks. "But if we turned up with blocks of gold, somebody'd hang us sure. Leastways they'd confiscate it, wouldn't they?"

"They would if they caught us with it anytime soon. We must see to it that they don't. Hide it in a safe place for a while. Years, if need be, till things in the country cool down again." As he spoke, Bridgeford was lifting out bars of gold. Three for Hawks; three for himself. He put the bricks in his haversack, leaving on the ground the half a canteen he'd used as a dinner plate, some hardtack, and a cast-iron frying pan. "Once the country cools down a bit from this war, we can go back for our buried gold and figure out a way to cash it in. There's jewelers in Wilmington that might help me out with that. We'd better get going, though, before it gets to be full day. I'd hate to lose my newfound fortune to Mr. Semple now."

"Where are we going?" asked Hawks, looking away down the empty white road.

Bridgeford hoisted himself into the saddle and trotted off toward the woods. "Our separate ways, Hawks," he said. "And may the good Lord take a liking to you."

Edinburgh

Dear Bill,

So now you have helped Dad move out of the house. How charming. I'm glad to see that you're making yourself useful. I wouldn't want our parents (who will have been married for twenty-nine years this August) to have any difficulties in dissolving their marriage and destroying our family. But why stop with that? Since you're being so helpful, couldn't you introduce him to a couple of stewardesses? Or rent him a room in a sorority? I've tried to write Dad myself, but I always end up tearing up the letter. I just get so furious that the letter becomes a stream of invective (not unlike the ones you've been receiving, only less restrained), and even I realize that if I mailed them they would only make matters worse.

Since you aren't married, you probably don't feel all the subtle overtones of this nightmare. For you, it's just a parental breakup, regrettable, of course, but hardly traumatic for a post-college adult. For me, though, it's something else again. I have not only lost my parents as parents, but also my sense of security in my marriage. I love Cameron, and everything be-

tween us seems perfectly fine—but is it? Can I ever really be sure of that? Does anybody really love anybody? And is it even possible these days for a relationship to last a lifetime? See, I don't know anymore.

If our parents' marriage, which I thought was the ultimate model of a safe and loving partnership, is flawed, then how can I trust my own? If they can fail, so can I. Perhaps, since I was raised by their example, I don't even know how to be happily married. Maybe I'm genetically programmed to fail. But I want my marriage to succeed. I couldn't stand losing Cameron, too—not after all this. And the worst part is that I can never, never be sure it won't happen. Ten years . . . twenty years . . . It's no guarantee. Suddenly marriage seems less like happily ever after and more like a time bomb: you don't know when it's going to explode in your face, but you can be pretty sure that it will.

I haven't really discussed this with Cameron. He says I worry too much. I'm quite depressed about it all, though. I admit that. I've stopped bothering about job hunting. Now I just sit around the apartment all day, reading silly novels with happy endings. Cameron says that I ought to go home if I'm going to brood about it so much, but I can't. This is one autopsy I simply cannot face.

Love (whatever that is),
Elizabeth

"Get there first with the most."
—GENERAL NATHAN BEDFORD
FORREST'S ADVICE
ON WINNING BATTLES

CHAPTER

5

BILL MACPHERSON SLIPPED OUT of his office and helped himself to a cup of coffee from the coffeemaker in the reception area.

"I thought you hated coffee," said Edith, waving a packet of Nutra Sweet, which he declined.

Bill glanced at his office door, which he had shut behind him. "I do hate it!" he hissed. "This was an excuse to come out here. I just wanted to tell you that if there are any calls, please interrupt me. Anybody at all. Even a wrong number."

Edith raised her eyebrows. "I thought you were conferring with a client."

"You mean, as opposed to having a family reunion? I am. I'm trying to fill out the Petition for Dissolution of Marriage with my mother, but it's tough going. I found myself looking forward to a call from Mr. Trowbridge. So feel free to interrupt."

"I'll keep that in mind," said Edith.

Bill looked into the other office. The door was open and no one sat at the tidy oak desk. The sight did nothing to improve his disposition. "Where's Powell? Isn't she here yet?"

"She had a date with Harry Wooding," said Edith solemnly.

"With who? Oh. You mean she's at the courthouse." Bill suddenly remembered that this was the name on the statue of a former mayor of Danville, situated on a landing of the courthouse steps. "Again? What do I have to do to see my own law partner?"

"You might try getting yourself arrested. Did you see her on the six o'clock news last night?"

"No. Was she discussing the murder case?"

"Yes. She looked real good. Had on that new linen blazer she bought at the mall, but they ran a piece on the crime before they interviewed her, and it sounded like the guy was guilty. But she's working hard to defend him. I sure do hope they're paying her by the hour for this case."

"Well, maybe the publicity will generate some business. It isn't as if we're swamped around here." He looked furtively at his office door. "I guess I'd better go back." With a sigh of martyrdom, he went back to his conference. "Here I am, Mother!" he said with all the forced cheerfulness he could muster. "You're sure you won't have some coffee?"

Margaret MacPherson sighed. "Caffeine is bad for you," she announced. "I never drink it anymore. You ought to get in some herbal tea instead."

"I'll look into it," Bill promised. A month ago he might have argued the point, but now he thought his mother might need all the deference that he could muster. "Shall we get on with this form?" he said gently. "It's just routine, you know, but as petitioner for the divorce, you and I have to fill in all the answers and file it with the County Circuit Court."

On his desk was the green loose-leaf notebook entitled *The Virginia Lawyer*, Bill's legal lifeline into the intricacies of his new profession. He picked up his yellow legal pad and tried to decipher what he had written. "Now, where were we?"

"We established that your father and I have both been residents of the state for more than a hundred and eighty days."

"'. . . preceding the filing of this petition.'" Bill nodded. "And we had your age and county of residence. Number three is Dad's age, place of employment, and county of residence. I'll fill that in." He scribbled more notes and consulted the form again. "Date and place of marriage?"

His mother twisted her hands in her lap and looked away. "August 23, 1961. Myrtle Beach, South Carolina. We eloped. My sister Amanda was furious with me. She had her heart set on a pastel-pink formal wedding, but I—well, it doesn't matter now. Go on to the next one."

Bill picked up the form and read aloud, "'Parties ceased co-habiting as husband and wife as of (insert date here), and separated and ceased living together as husband and wife on (insert date here.)'" He was careful not to look up from the paper as he finished reading.

After a palpable silence, Bill's mother said, "He moved out two weeks ago, wasn't it? On a Saturday."

"Uh—yes," muttered Bill. "That's the ceased-living-together part. I'll need a date for the other one, too."

"Could I have some of that coffee now?" asked Margaret MacPherson.

◆　◆　◆

NATHAN KIMBALL HAD SPENT most of the past two days boning up on Virginia real estate law and double-checking his client's proposed purchase. While he was thus occupied with legal business, John Huff spent his time playing tourist, although what he could have found to view after the first hour was a mystery to his attorney.

Huff drove his rental car out to Lucktown, north of Danville, to look at a historical marker on the site of the old railroad depot. Rejecting Bill MacPherson's suggestions of various local motels, he took rooms for himself and his attorney in an ornate Queen Anne–style bed and breakfast on the elegant section of Main Street known locally as Millionaire's Row. He took long walks in the warm June sunshine, admiring the late Victorian houses that line Danville's grandest old thoroughfare. In these graceful old mansions the city's tobacco and textile barons had entertained each other—and even generated a bit of minor history. On the corner of Main and Broad streets was the birthplace of the Langhorne sisters; Nancy became Viscountess Astor, the first woman to sit in Britain's House of Commons, and her sister Irene became the model for the Gibson Girl, created by her artist-husband, Charles Dana Gibson.

Huff spent a good bit of time in one of the oldest houses on Main Street, once the residence of William T. Sutherlin and now the Danville Museum of Fine Arts and History. For a week in April 1865, the massive gray sandstone building topped with a glass cupola had been the last capitol of the Confederacy, sheltering Jefferson Davis and his cabinet after the fall of Richmond. Huff wandered around the rooms of restored Victorian furnishings, with plaster ceiling work and its elaborately carved furniture. He told the curator that he was thinking of buying an antebellum home, and that he needed ideas on how to decorate it. However, he spent a good bit of time reading Jefferson Davis's last speech, penned in the drawing room. And he asked if there were any local memoirs dating from the Civil War in the library upstairs. He paid scant attention to the displays of quilts and local artwork in the basement of the museum, but he was most interested in finding out whether there had been any additions to the house in modern times—and where outbuildings had stood a century before.

When Nathan Kimball returned to the bed and breakfast at four o'clock, he found Mr. Huff sitting in the chair by the window reading local-history pamphlets with the air of someone studying for an exam. He looked up as the door opened. "Well?"

Kimball, who had long given up expecting courtesy from his client, ignored the brusqueness of the salutation. "Everything seems to check out," he said, loosening his tie as he sat down on the bed. "Though, of course, if you were relying on bank financing, they'd want to do everything about three times, just to make sure. Still, I've looked over MacPherson's paperwork—title search, the terms of the deed, and so on. The house was left as a trust for the widows and daughters of Confederate veterans, but there was a clause stating that the board—that is, the residents and their attorney—could dispose of the house if it was no longer needed for its original purpose. I think it's safe to assume that there won't be any more widows or daughters turning up at this late date."

"Not after a hundred and thirty-odd years," Huff agreed.

"I mentioned that we were thinking of offering a million two, and he said he'd talk to his clients, but that he thought that they'd wait for other offers in that case. Apparently they have received other responses to their ad."

Huff narrowed his eyes. "On whose authority did you offer them less than the asking price?"

"Well, I didn't think you'd mind," stammered Kimball. "I thought I might save you some money, since the sellers seem to be in a hurry, and you once said you expected a discount for cash."

"Tell MacPherson we'll meet their price. But we want to close tomorrow."

◆ ◆ ◆

THE WALK FROM the law office to the police station took A. P. Hill up Loyal Street, past an old tobacco warehouse that was once Confederate Prison No. 6. Sometimes she would linger, looking at the old building, remembering the harrowing account she had read of conditions in Danville's military prisons. Today, though, her thoughts were on the more modern version of prison in Danville: the jail in which Tug Mosier awaited trial, unable to make bail.

She had examined the police reports about the murder of Misti Hale, but the results seemed inconclusive. They had been unable to locate any of Tug's drinking buddies from the evening in question, and no witnesses saw him or anyone else enter his home that night. Misti Hale had been strangled, and there was no physical evidence—hairs, fingerprints, or anything else—to identify her killer. The evidence against Tug Mosier was circumstantial, but as she had learned in law school, many a man has been hanged on circumstantial evidence. (Well, been electrocuted, then, since this was Virginia.) If the prosecutor could find a motive or convince a jury that he had planned the crime in advance, he could be convicted of capital murder. In theory, Powell Hill did not disapprove of the death penalty, but in practice, she didn't want to feel eternally responsible if her client paid the extreme penalty because her defense was not adequate.

Tug Mosier's past did not help matters either. As his attorney, Powell could not present him to a jury as an upstanding citizen who had accidentally fallen under suspicion of a crime through no fault of his own. Mosier was an eleventh-grade dropout whose checkered job record seldom showed anything lasting longer than a year or paying more than minimum wage. He came from a broken home and had run away from his grandmother's care by the time he was fifteen. The grandmother had been dead for years now, and apparently there was no one else who cared what happened to Tug Mosier.

He had a string of run-ins with the law that stretched all the way back to junior high school: throwing bricks off the overpass and trying to hit passing cars. From there he progressed to drunk driving, assault charges for barroom fights, and an occasional larceny or bad-check charge. He had served time in various county jails, but never in prison. All in all, his criminal record presented a picture of an irresponsible man lacking in ambition and self-control, one with a penchant for violence—just the sort of man who could have killed Misti Hale in a drunken argument. Worst of all, Tug Mosier was not even proclaiming his innocence; all he could offer was a reasonable doubt about his own guilt. Powell Hill wondered if she could persuade a jury to give him the benefit of that doubt, considering his record.

The television news story last night hadn't helped, either. The news team had begun with a shot of an unshaven Tug Mosier, dressed in jeans and an undershirt, leering at the camera. Then they had cut to an interview with the grieving family of Misti Hale. *They* looked as worthy and upstanding as the Waltons, expressing their sorrow in dignified tones. Misti had been the wayward daughter of a well-liked local pediatrician. Dr. Hale's colleagues, friends, and former patients would naturally be outraged by the murder of his pretty daughter. Powell could imagine the television audience chanting: *Guilty! Guilty! Guilty!* The story made headlines in the morning paper, too. She wondered if there was anybody left in Danville who didn't think that Tug Mosier was a human pit bull.

A. P. Hill had walked another half block before that thought came around again, and this time she really considered its implications. Would there be local prejudice in the case? Enough to jeopardize her client's right to a fair trial? She decided that before she went back to talk to Tug, she'd better go to the courthouse and find a Silverback. She had to find out how to go about getting a change of venue for Tug Mosier's murder trial.

◆ ◆ ◆

BILL MACPHERSON WAS UP to his ears in tedious paperwork and silence was worth four dollars a minute, so naturally the phone rang. The trill of the bell so close to his ear annoyed him so much that he snatched it up at once, forgetting about Edith in the outer office.

"Hello! MacPherson and Hill."

"Is that you, Bill?" The drawling tones of an elderly voice froze Bill as he sat gripping the phone. "I just had a little question. Thought I'd put you on it."

"That's what I'm here for," he managed to say. "How are you, Mr. Trowbridge?"

"Oh, I can't complain." *I'll bet you can*, thought Bill. "Well, here's my question. Have you got a pencil handy to jot this down?"

"Ready when you are," said Bill, striving to keep a note of impatience out of his voice.

"Well, I was just wondering. I was watching a cop show on television last night. Suppose a policeman arrested a guy who had a fake ID. Say he was calling himself Fred Jones when his real name was Bob Brown. So the arrest papers and everything will be made out in the phony name. Can the guy go all the way through the trial and sentencing and then produce identification to say who he really is, then claim that the charges don't apply to him because he was misidentified? Can he tell them to go find somebody named Fred Jones and put him in jail? Can he do that?"

Bill blinked. "No. We didn't cover that in law school, but I'm pretty sure it wouldn't work. You may be able to outsmart the state, but not as easily as that. I suppose you want me to check on it formally, though."

"Sure, I'd like to know exactly *why* it wouldn't work. You could look it up."

"Yeah. Okay. I'll see what I can do." Bill sighed. "Give me a couple of days. I'll call you back."

"That's fine," said Trowbridge cheerfully. "You know, this is a lot of fun. It's one of the best presents the wife has ever come up with."

What did she give you last year? thought Bill. *A thumbscrew?* Aloud he said, "I'll be in touch, Mr. Trowbridge. Goodbye."

The next time the phone rang, about two minutes later, Bill had no trouble remembering to let Edith answer it. Seconds later she appeared in the doorway. "Nathan Kimball for you," she said. "Good luck."

Bill motioned for her to stay. "Yes?" he said into the phone. "Yes, this is he . . . All right . . . Yes, I understand . . . Tomorrow? But that's a lot of paperwork . . . I see. Well, if you put it that way. I suppose we could—I'll tell my clients and call you back. Ten minutes or so . . . Good. Until then." He hung up the phone with a bemused smile. "You want the good news, Edith, or the bad news?"

"Give me the good news," said Edith. "It'll make a nice change."

"Mr. Huff has decided to buy the Home for Confederate Women. His lawyers have okayed the deal, and he's willing to pay the asking price without any quibbling." Bill looked smug. "I mentioned that there had been other inquiries."

"You mean the old guy who wanted to see it if we'd trade it for $65,000 and a trailer at Virginia Beach?"

"Well, it *was* an offer of sorts," said Bill.

"Okay. The good news is Mr. Huff will buy the house for the asking price. And the bad news is—what? He wants to pay it in Confederate money?" asked Edith.

"No. The bad news is that we have to close the deal tomorrow."

Edith sneered. "That's impossible. When my brother bought his house, it liked to have taken forever."

"That was because he needed bank financing," Bill told her. "Mortgages do take forever. But if Mr. Huff is paying cash—well, not *cash*, but transferring funds from his bank to ours, without borrowing any money from anyone—then all we have to do is the paperwork."

"That must be the bad news," said Edith. "That's a lot of documents to generate in one day's time. I suppose you'll be wanting me to cancel my evening's plans and work overtime."

"I really need you," said Bill. "But we'll be able to afford to pay you overtime from our commission from the sale of the house."

"Well, that's good. It's nice to know that I could afford to eat if I ever had the time. I'd better get started on it. Have you called the old ladies yet?"

"That's my next move," said Bill, reaching for the phone. "Just think! I've finished my first case. Won't Powell be pleased?"

"You bet. And astonished, too," said Edith, strolling back to her desk.

It's amazing how much time lawyers spend on the phone, Bill thought as he dialed the Home for Confederate Women. *Gab and write letters.* After four rings, the receiver was picked up, and Bill heard Flora Dabney's voice. "Miss Dabney! Bill MacPherson here. I have wonderful news! Mr. Huff wants to buy your house. Tomorrow!"

Five minutes later Bill was standing in front of Edith's desk, with an expression of utter dismay.

Edith looked up from her computer terminal. "Well? She hasn't changed her mind about selling, has she?"

"No," said Bill, perching on the edge of the desk. "It's not as bad as that. It's just that she says they can't come to the office tomorrow. Apparently, one of them has a doctor's appointment, and another one isn't feeling well enough to leave the house. I explained to her that Mr. Huff wants to finalize the sale tomorrow."

"And what did she say?"

"She wants me to handle the whole thing."

"Don't they want to meet this fellow who's buying their house?"

"Apparently not. We finally decided that I would draw up a power of attorney form and go over there now and get it signed. Then at the closing tomorrow, I'll sign the papers on their behalf."

"Who gets the money, then?"

"Mr. Huff gives me a cashier's check or wires the funds or whatever, and it gets deposited in the firm's trust account. Then I deduct our commission, and pay the rest to Miss Dabney and her housemates. So that won't change."

"Did you remember to call Mr. Kimball and tell him that tomorrow is all set?"

"Yeah, just now," said Bill. "I also asked him about defendants who use phony names, but he was no help."

"What?"

"Never mind. Just another one of Mr. Trowbridge's questions. I'd better get going now if I want to get all this done. I'll be back as soon as I can. Want me to bring back a pizza?"

"Are you buying?"

"Yes," said Bill. "Company expenses."

"Then bring back two pizzas," said Edith. "I'll need all my strength to complete this paperwork."

◆   ◆   ◆

After a frantic scramble through the reference books, Bill managed to find the power-of-attorney instructions, type them up on his computer, and produce a presentable-looking printout to take with him to the Home for Confederate Women. As he drove out Highway 58 toward the old mansion, he tried to remember everything he knew about real estate transactions, just to make sure that he wasn't over-looking anything. It seemed simple enough. He'd be glad to get this case out of the way; perhaps then he could get a more interesting one. He was a little jealous of his partner's newfound importance as the defender of an accused murderer. And what was Bill doing? Paperwork in a divorce and answering stupid questions for Calvin Trowbridge. He would also be glad to finalize the house sale because, as unexciting as it was, it would be his first case, successfully completed; then he could feel that he was really a lawyer.

He turned down the quiet country road that led to the white-columned mansion, enjoying the country scenery, golden in the late afternoon sun, and thinking how pleasant it was that his first lawyerly duty should be an act of benevolent service for a group of sweet, helpless old ladies.

◆   ◆   ◆

In the mahogany dining room Flora Dabney had assembled the other residents of the home for a conference. She explained to them that Bill MacPherson ("That nice young man!") had succeeded in finding a buyer for the house, and that the sale would take place tomorrow. "I thought it best for us not to attend personally," she said. "So I've asked Bill to come out here and bring a power-of-attorney form for us to sign. That way he can represent us at the actual closing, and we need not be present."

Ellen Morrison looked up with a worried frown. "But how will we be paid? Can we trust this lawyer?"

"He's very young, dear," said Mary Lee Pendleton. "I'm sure he wouldn't dream of defrauding helpless old ladies."

"There was a Union general called McPherson in the War," Lydia Bridgeford pointed out. Her interest in genealogy occasionally spilled over into other people's antecedents.

"I believe they spell it differently," said Flora Dabney. "At any rate, the buyer is paying cash, so the money should be ours within the week. Of course that means we shall have to move out rather quickly. I'm sure the gentleman will want to take possession without delay."

Julia Hotchkiss watched silently from her wheelchair with a bag of Fig Newtons wrapped in her lap robe. She waited for signs of refreshments, and when none were forthcoming, she eased a cookie out of the folds of the blanket and, when she thought no one was looking, stuffed it in her cheek.

"The important thing is that the money be safe," said Ellen Morrison. "I lived through the Great Depression once, and I don't mean to live hand to mouth ever again. I've been seeing in the paper about these banks going under and whatnot, and I just don't know that I trust them."

Flora Dabney and Dolly Smith looked at each other. "That's quite true, Ellen," Flora said after a moment's pause. "It is important that the money be safe, because at our age we are not likely to come by much more of it. I discussed that very point with Mary Lee when we first decided to go through with this."

"Yes," said Mary Lee Pendleton. "I knew just who to ask. You know that nice young fellow who comes by to take me to church? He's in banking. So about a month ago I asked him what would be a really safe place to put money, and of course he said that his bank was as secure as they come. But I laughed and said that I had been watching a television program, and that the people on the show made a lot of money in a shady way, and they did something else with it." She blushed. "I'm afraid I fibbed about the TV program, but it was in a good cause."

"Well?" said Dolly Smith impatiently. "What did he say?"

"At first he talked about money laundering. I never could make head nor tails of his explanation—so I said I didn't think that was it. Finally, as we were pulling into the church parking lot, he laughed—in that superior way men have—and he said, 'Well, Miss Mary, you could always stash your ill-gotten gains in a numbered account in the Cayman Islands. They won't tell anybody who's got what.' "

"What in the world are the Cayman Islands?" asked Anna Douglas from the doorway. As usual, she was late for the meeting.

"They're in the Caribbean," said Mary Lee. "Not that it matters, because you don't have to go there, although I'm sure they're very nice. All I had to do was telephone a bank there and ask to set up an account, and I sent them a check."

"For how much?" asked Lydia Bridgeford. "We can't spare much."

"Sixty-five dollars," said Mary Lee. "Half of that was Flora's. We bought a money order at the 7-Eleven and sent it in."

"In your name?" asked Ellen. "But what if something happens to you? How will we get the money?"

"All you need is the account number and the paperwork. They explained it all to me. You just use the number for transactions. Besides, I opened the account in a different name altogether. Mrs. James Ewell Brown Stuart."

Lydia Bridgeford nodded approvingly. "Jeb Stuart, eh? I expect he'd rather like that. After all, he was born in the next county over, so he is rather a neighbor of ours."

"Except of course that he's dead," said Mary Lee Pendleton.

"At Yellow Tavern in 1864," sighed Flora, who had rather a thing about the late general.

"I'd hardly have opened an account for him if he weren't dead," snapped Mary Lee. "The whole point is that we have to hang on to this money. It's all we've got for our old age."

"Well, perhaps not," said Dolly Smith.

◆　◆　◆

"YOU WANT ME TO DO WHAT with the money?" asked Bill MacPherson, staring at the circle of smiling pink faces.

"It's very simple," Flora Dabney assured him. "I expect you haven't done that sort of transaction before, but there's really nothing to worry about. You simply instruct your bank to wire it to this account number at *our* bank, which happens to be in the Cayman Islands."

"But why do you want the money wired to a Caribbean island?" wailed Bill.

"We thought we might go there," said Dolly Smith. "My doctor said it might help my arthritis."

"But why deposit the money there? They take traveler's checks in the Caymans."

Flora Dabney smiled. "Well, it's a little embarrassing. Will you promise not to laugh if we confide in you?"

Bill nodded.

"Well, it's just that we felt a little funny about selling *Confederate* property and putting the money in a U.S. bank. I know that when I first hired you I said that the war was over, but some of the ladies here still feel strongly about it. Very strongly."

"My dear papa never believed in banks after '29," said Ellen Morrison. "And I believe most of them are controlled out of New York, which just goes to show you."

"And since there is no longer a Confederacy, we decided to send the money out of the country altogether."

Bill stared at his clients. Surely they were joking. "But what if you want to use some of it? To buy groceries and things!"

"In that case," said Flora, "we might find it necessary to transfer some of it back. But for now you must allow us our little gesture. Now here's the account number. Don't lose it."

"Wasn't there something else you wanted?" asked Anna Douglas. "I'm late for bridge club."

"Oh, the power of attorney," said Bill, recalling his original errand. "I drew up a form authorizing me to act on your behalf in the selling of the property. I need each of you to sign on these lines." He pointed out the appropriate place on the document, and produced the pen his parents had given him for graduation. One by one the ladies signed their names, passing the pen from hand to hand: Flora Dabney, Mary Lee Pendleton, Ellen Morrison, Lydia Bridgeford, Anna Douglas, and Dolly Hawks Smith. Julia Hotchkiss had to be persuaded to sign by the offer of another package of cookies, but in the end she scrawled her name below Jenny Allan's tentative script, and the form was complete.

"I guess that's it," said Bill, putting the paper back in his briefcase.

"Tomorrow Mr. Huff will come to my office, and we'll sign the deed. After that you'll have two weeks to vacate the house. Will that be sufficient?"

"Oh, yes," said Mary Lee Pendleton with her serene smile. "We have already decided to go to Oakmont, that lovely retirement community just outside town. They have charming little apartments and a dining hall and people to check on you if you need anything. We'll still be together."

Flora Dabney patted his arm. "And you must come out and see us. Perhaps you could come to tea in a month or so, when we're settled."

"Thank you," said Bill. "I'll try to do that."

"And you won't forget about depositing the money, will you?" asked Ellen Morrison.

"It will go straight from the firm's trust account to you. Less my commission, of course. I'm one of the honest lawyers," said Bill.

They all laughed merrily.

Forty-five minutes later Bill returned to the office with two large pizzas balanced on the top of his briefcase. "How's it going?" he called to Edith. "Any problems?"

"Maybe one," said Edith, clearing space on her desk for the pizzas. "Did you get the old ladies to sign that power-of-attorney form?"

"I sure did," said Bill. "See? Eight signatures."

"Uh-huh." Edith frowned as she examined the form. "Did you remember to have a notary present?"

"Oh, shit!"

"Shall I take that as a no?"

Bill sat down and put his head in his hands. "I completely forgot," he groaned. "I was so busy rushing around, trying to get back here and finish the rest of this paperwork and buy the pizzas and all. It just slipped my mind."

Edith sighed. "Want me to type up another one?"

"Well, one of the ladies said she had bridge club tonight. I might not be able to get all the signatures. Oh, hell. I should have thought to take you along. You're a notary, aren't you?"

"Yes," said Edith, cutting the pizza with her letter opener. "Did you remember the napkins?"

"No. Use a paper towel. Look, I don't suppose you could notarize this now, could you? I mean, I know you're supposed to see the document being signed, but I *swear* to you that they all signed it, and I signed it, and it's all legal. Oh, please, Edith! If we don't get all this done by tomorrow, the deal will fall through."

Over a slice of pepperoni pizza, Edith gave him a look of exasperation. "All right," she said. "You are new at this. I guess everybody's entitled to one incredibly stupid screwup. But it's illegal, you hear? So I don't want you ever to make this mistake again." She opened her desk drawer, took out her notary seal, and witnessed the document.

"Thanks, Edith," said Bill. "I promise I'll never forget again. You've saved my life."

"That'll be a dollar," said Edith.

◆ ◆ ◆

RADFORD, VIRGINIA

THERE WERE ONLY SIX gray-clad soldiers in a makeshift camp near the house. The redbrick mansion sat on a hill overlooking the New River; it had belonged to a colonel in the Revolutionary War. Now its sprawling green lawn was dotted again with tents and tethered horses.

On the hill all was quiet. Beneath a tarp stretched across four poles, one grizzled sergeant spread out a makeshift dinner of hardtack, apples, and potatoes. On a log in front of the tent, a lanky bearded soldier was cleaning a rifle and passing the time of day with a rawboned mountain boy, who was whittling on a stick of applewood. The smallest Rebel, a baby-faced corporal with wire-rimmed spectacles, was sitting on the edge of the hill beside the small cannon. The corporal was making ammunition cartridges by pouring gunpowder into paper tubes to be fired at some forthcoming battle. At the bottom of the hill, a private in a makeshift uniform was walking the perimeter, pacing back and forth with his rifle on his shoulder, solemn and silent. The group's commanding officer, a stocky red-bearded man who in civilian life was a country lawyer, sat with his back against an oak tree, making notes in a small leather book.

The homemade flag flapping in the breeze read THE WYTHE GRAYS and in smaller block letters beneath it: 68th VIRGINIA INFANTRY. The flagstaff was a six-foot tree limb, trimmed of its branches, but gnarled, and still bearing gray bark. It was propped against a cheval-de-frise, a log pierced by sharp sticks used as a defensive barricade. Beside the regimental flag flew the Southern Battle Flag, a red field crossed by two blue stripes emblazoned with stars. It was the only Confederate flag that most people ever saw, but it was not the flag of the nation; the Southern equivalent of the U.S. Stars and Stripes was the Stars and Bars, a circle of seven stars on a square of blue, with two broad red strips separated by a band of white. It was not particularly distinctive, and like President Jefferson Davis, it would be all but forgotten after the war, while Robert E. Lee and his star-crossed battle flag lived on in song and story.

"Do you need any help, Corporal?" The grizzled sergeant had finished laying out the food and wandered over to observe the cartridge-making.

"Nice of you to ask, now that I'm about finished. Think we'll need more than that?"

"Depends on what transpires this afternoon. If nobody shows up, one of us may have to galvanize. Unless you want to sit around all afternoon and bake in that wool uniform."

"How about galvanizing Randy? He's been on guard duty for a good while. He deserves a little excitement."

"Okay. We'll see. It's early yet. Might as well wait a while."

"Are you expecting any action, Sergeant Jennings?"

"Maybe. The 15th U.S. knows we're here." From the edge of the hill, he looked out across the little town of Radford, where all was quiet on the summer afternoon.

Suddenly the sentry shouted, "Company coming!" and they all looked down toward the bottom of the hill, where a white Ford Tempo was pulling into the municipal parking lot.

"Places everybody!" yelled the red-bearded officer. "Civilians on the way!"

The civilians, a yuppie family with two small children, got out and made their way up the hill. The little boy, a sturdy blond who looked about four, ran over to inspect the cannon from a cautious distance, while his parents and older sister looked at the food display under the tarpaulin. "But Arby's is just across the street," said the little girl, a prim nine-year-old firmly in the bossy stage of childhood.

"Arby's?" echoed Sergeant Jennings in tones of complete bewilderment. "What's that, little lady?"

The child pointed to the fast-food place beyond the parking lot and across the street. "That restaurant. We just had lunch there."

"All I see are some houses," said the sergeant peering out in the direction of her pointing. "And if one of them is owned by a Mr. Arby, we'd sure be happy if he'd bring us some grub, but we haven't heard tell of him."

"They have to stay in character, Megan," said the little girl's mother. "Remember it's supposed to be 1862 for them."

"1864, ma'am," Jennings replied.

The little girl looked at the sergeant's uniform and wrinkled her freckled nose. "There's a dry cleaner's over there across the road, too, mister."

After a few moments of silence the little boy ventured to speak to the corporal, who was still sitting near the cannon. "Hey, is that thing real?"

"Sure is," the corporal replied. "We might fire in a couple of minutes, in case you're interested. What's your name?"

"Josh. You gonna shoot anything?"

"Not with cannon balls, but it'll make a loud booming noise. You'll like it."

Josh considered this for a moment, and then turned his attention to the corporal. "Those are funny shoes."

"They're Jefferson brogans. That's what you wear if you're a Confederate soldier."

"Is that a real gun?"

"It sure is. It's an 1841 Springfield smooth-bore musket. I was just making cartridges for it. See?"

"Did you ever kill anybody?"

"Umm. In a battle it's hard to tell," said the corporal, and the little boy wandered away.

After a few more minutes of inspection and explanation, followed by the firing of the small cannon, a Yankee sniper (Randy, the sentry, now wearing a blue uniform) appeared. He fired blanks at the Rebel encampment and was chased around the old house for a tree-to-tree shoot-out. Finally, the young corporal took aim and brought down the sniper, who died dramatically and at great length near the visitors.

That little boy said, "Can I have his hat?"

Two of the soldiers carried the body behind the house, to change clothes and return to sentry duty, and the family left. The lanky soldier who had been cleaning his gun walked over to talk to the corporal.

"That little girl was tough," he laughed. "She kept trying to trip us up by asking about current events. Captain Nance handled her pretty well, though. I like talking to kids. The ones I hate are the know-it-alls." He assumed a pompous facial expression and mimicked such a civilian. "Soldier, that is a *navy* Colt pistol that you are wearing, not an army one!"

"I can usually come up with a plausible story," said the corporal. "There was all kinds of scrounging going on during the war. Hardly anybody was regulation past '63. The ones I hate are the people who assume that because we're Confederate reenactors we're redneck racists."

"Just remind them that it was Philip Sheridan, the *Union* general, who said, 'The only good Indian is a dead Indian,' when the army sent him out West after the war."

"I'm not supposed to know that," said the corporal. "It hasn't happened yet!"

"Oh, that's right. Well, you could go into a long explanation about states' rights and representative voting by population and import tariffs, but people have never found those explanations very glamorous. That's why the North always claimed the war was a crusade, even though the

Emancipation Proclamation wasn't issued until halfway through the war. People like easy, flashy answers to complicated issues."

"I know, Ken. Usually, I just say I'm a corporal from the mountains, and that I don't know anything about politics."

Ken shook his head. "You're a corporal. Boy, is that ironic."

"You think I should be playing my own great-grandfather like you're doing, right? Well, I can't do that. I would be way too conspicuous. And the Silverbacks would never stand for it."

"The what?"

"The good old boys who run things. They may not be racists, but they sure as hell can be chauvinists. That's why I keep a low profile. And that's why you can't tell anybody who I am."

"But you're a good reenactor," said Ken Filban. "Do you really think they'd mind?"

"Mind?" said A. P. Hill. "They'd go ballistic."

CHAPTER
6

JOHN HUFF STOOD in the front hall of his newly purchased home, savoring the emptiness and the echoes of his own footsteps. The old ladies were gone, taking with them all their furniture and knick-knacks, but leaving a tantalizing collection of trunks and boxes in the basement. He'd already checked. It was the first place he went. Well, not the *first* place; it had been a long drive out from the airport and he'd had two whiskey sodas on the plane; but after that, it was his first concern. He could examine the papers themselves later. The electricity was still on and the house's water supply came from a well, so there was no billing problem to interrupt service there either. It was only three o'clock; the moving van should be arriving any minute with his furniture. With any luck and a little hustle on the part of the movers (which he would see to personally) he would be able to spend the night in his new residence. He had got a good deal on the house, he thought for the hundredth time. These Southern yokels were no match for a businessman of his caliber.

Apart from his other interests in Danville, he thought that the house might make a very nice vacation home; perhaps even a place to retire to. He was bored with the usual vacation spots frequented by his acquaintances. He was getting a little old for skiing, and thoughts of skin cancer dimmed his enjoyment of the beach. He had been divorced for years, and there were no children to consider in his vacation preferences. He could please himself. Perhaps a graceful Victorian mansion was the perfect retreat for a gentleman of his age and income. He might even take up fox hunting. After the completion of his current project, that is.

He looked appraisingly at the silent rooms, with sunlight filtering through the curtainless windows making dust motes dance above the oak plank floors. There was no sensation of the lingering dead haunting the empty halls. Too bad, thought Huff with a wry smile; he would have welcomed a couple of ghosts. He would have had questions to pose to them.

After a last look around, while he mentally arranged his furniture in these graceful rooms, John Huff sat down on the stairs to wait for the moving van.

◆　◆　◆

FOR PERHAPS the fiftieth time since he began his law practice, Bill MacPherson considered the idea of raising sheep. Sheep were so restful. So pleasantly bland. They just stood around all day not arguing with anybody, not asking silly questions, and not minding that a dozen ewes all had to share the same ram. You never heard of a sheep filing for divorce; no sirree bob. They just stood around in their fields, placidly content with whatever mate was provided for them. Sheep never went off to find themselves. Bill pictured himself out on a green hillside with a clever collie (sort of a canine A. P. Hill), communing with nature, soaking up sunshine, and counting his lamb chops.

He was jerked back to fluorescent reality by the sound of his mother's voice, containing all the warmth of an injured timber wolf. "He's driving me crazy!" she wailed.

Bill closed his eyes and ran his hands through his hair, wondering whether he was supposed to respond as a son or as a lawyer. He opted for the second choice, thinking that the emotional distance of the attorney-client relationship might make for a calmer discussion. "All right, Mother," he said gently. "Take it easy. What has Dad done now?"

"He keeps coming back to the house, saying he forgot something. Last week he took the road atlas, the flashlight, and the sea-shell ashtray you made at 4-H camp."

"What did he want that for? I thought he quit smoking."

"I don't know. Maybe he's too cheap to buy cereal bowls. What does it matter? I don't want him wandering in and out of the house. And that's not the worst of it! He's killing the fish."

"The fish?"

"The goldfish. Doug used to always accuse me of forgetting to feed the goldfish, and now he is convinced that they'll starve unless he dumps food into the tank. But since I feed them every morning, the food he adds is more than they need. I can always tell when he's been in the house—even before I look to see what's missing—because there's a little bloated body floating on top of the water."

"Okay," sighed Bill. "So you want him to stay away from the house. Have you told him?"

"Yes. He always says it's the last time. He says he just forgot one little thing. And then three days later he's back. Sometimes he comes when I'm out, and I panic and think a burglar has broken in, but the dead fish give him away."

"What does he say about killing the fish?"

"Natural causes. He suggests an autopsy."

"Do you want me to talk to him?"

Margaret MacPherson hesitated. "Can I have him arrested for trespassing?"

"No, Mother, you cannot have him arrested. Why don't you just change the locks?"

"Because I can't remember who all has keys! Elizabeth does, and you do, and I think Robert and Amanda have one set. Oh, it would be too much trouble to change all the locks and redistribute keys. Besides, why should I have to go to all that trouble and expense? Can't I just have your father arrested?"

Bill closed his eyes and thought about fields of cloudlike sheep. "Okay," he said at last, "if you insist on indulging in legal carpet bombing, I will handle it. We will file a restraining order against Dad, specifying that he cannot come into the house to retrieve anything without your express permission, and that he cannot enter the premises unless you are present." Bill was scribbling notes to himself on the yellow legal pad.

"Don't forget the fish!"

"Right. The fish. The restraining order will absolutely prohibit Douglas W. MacPherson from feeding any and all fish at his former residence at 816 Mead Lane. I'll get it typed up and formally present it to Dad's lawyer. Will that do?"

Bill's mother gave him a reproachful look. "You don't have to take that tone with me, Bill. I'll have you know that it's very stressful to have an estranged husband popping in and out of your house like Banquo's ghost, and besides, I happen to be very fond of those goldfish. We'd had the fantail moor for almost three years."

"I'll put that in the restraining order. Maybe it will mute the hilarity."

"Will your father and I have to go to court over this?"

"No, I don't think so," said Bill, who hadn't filed a restraining order before. "His lawyer will have to appear, though. And I'll be there."

"But if he ignores the restraining order and barges in anyway, *then* we can have him arrested?"

"Well, theoretically. I think if it's just a case of fish murder, the judge might let him go with a scolding. He might order Dad to replace the fish."

"Impossible!" snapped Margaret MacPherson. "Doug can't swim."

They looked at each other and burst out laughing. It was the first symptom of sanity Bill had seen in any of his family members in weeks.

◆   ◆   ◆

JOHN HUFF STOOD on the front porch supervising the unloading of the moving van. "Be careful with that sofa!" he called out. "Don't scrape the upholstery against the door frame."

The movers swept past him without even pretending to heed his warning. "That goes in the room to the right!" he called after them. He got up and peered into the trunk to see how much furniture they had left to unload. The truck was still at least half full. They wouldn't finish until after five o'clock. He was glad he wasn't paying them by the hour.

The movers had just unloaded an antique walnut desk and were stumbling precariously up the steps with it when Huff's attention was deflected by the arrival of a white sedan pulling into the winding drive- way. Huff did not recognize the dark-haired young man behind the wheel; for a moment he had thought that it was the sellers' attorney Bill MacPherson, coming to welcome him to town, and perhaps to hustle a little future legal business. But while this young man looked like a lawyer, in his Southern prep's uniform of spotted tie and khaki slacks, he certainly didn't look like a welcoming committee. He was staring open-mouthed at the moving van and flipping through a sheaf of papers on a clipboard as he approached the house. *Local tax assessor,* thought John Huff, bracing himself for the confrontation. These yokels would soon learn that they couldn't push him around. Huff sat where he was and waited for Mr. Power Tie's opening salvo.

He didn't have long to wait. The young man looked at the moving van, jotted down its license plate, and said, "Well, my goodness, we're busy this afternoon." He waved his hand at the truck, the house, and John Huff. "And just what are we up to here?"

"Well, I'm moving into my new house, and you're trespassing," said Huff. He believed in asserting himself at the earliest possible moment.

The reply was an unconvincing imitation of a smile. "I beg your pardon? *I* am trespassing? Do you know who I am?"

"No, I can't help you there. Are you lost?"

The young man drew himself up to his full height—about five seven —and announced, "Sir, I am Randolph Custis Byrd, and I have the honor to be the assistant director of art and antiquities for the Commonwealth of Virginia. Now please tell me what is transpiring here. I thought the elderly ladies were going to wait for *us* to assist them in vacating the premises."

"They didn't wait. I guess with a million dollars they didn't need any help with moving expenses from the state."

R. Custis Byrd stared in disbelief. "A million dollars? Are you serious? But where would they . . ." He peered into the back of the moving van. "They didn't sell you the furniture, did they?"

"No," said Huff. "I didn't want it. I'd rather furnish the house to my own taste."

"Furnish the house?" echoed Byrd. "What are you talking about?" Two movers in gray coveralls clumped past them up the ramp and into the truck, and emerged balancing a recliner between them. Byrd watched them go with an expression of horror that the recliner's upholstery did not quite merit. "Why are you moving a lounge chair into the state art museum?"

Now it was John Huff's turn to look stricken. "Art museum? You must have come to the wrong house. Why, I paid a fortune for this house not two weeks ago!"

"I hope not. This was the Home for Confederate Women. The state has decided to claim it for the people of Virginia because of its historic value. I have the paperwork right here if you'd like to see it. In return for the house, we were planning to move the eight current residents to a nursing home outside Danville, and to pay for their care for the rest of their lives. The poor old dears ought to be on their way to Bingo Heaven right now. Where are they, by the way?"

John Huff set his jaw. "I tell you I bought this house."

"Well, you've been taken in by a fraud, sir," said Custis Byrd in tones bordering on sympathy. "Who sold it to you?"

"A Danville attorney named Bill MacPherson."

◆ ◆ ◆

A. P. HILL HAD RETURNED to the twentieth century, exchanging her gray infantry uniform for the navy-blue coat and skirt that was her legal uniform. Reenacting was an enjoyable hobby, and a way for her to feel closer to her great-great-grandfather the general, but the present-day A. P. Hill had no desire to live permanently in the past. The Spring-field rifle, the brogans, and the rimless spectacles had all been put away until next weekend's reenactment, a scripted skirmish to take place at a battlefield that was now a national park. Now she had to return to a more crucial battle: the trial of Tug Mosier.

Because of the local sentiment about the case and the fact that the victim came from a prominent family, Powell had succeeded in getting a change of venue. Now the trial was scheduled for the end of the month in Stuart, a small town in Patrick County, some fifty miles west of Danville. She hoped that the new location would filter some of the emotion out of the case. At least she would have jurors who weren't former classmates of Misti Hale or friends of the victim's parents.

Now she had to decide how best to proceed with the defense. She was consulting a possible expert witness, Dr. Arthur Timmons, a Rich-mond psychiatrist who had some experience in criminal cases. As Pow-ell Hill sat in his waiting room, leafing through old copies of *Smithso-nian*, she wondered which would prove the more difficult task: coming up with a way to help her client or persuading a prominent physician to consult for nothing.

He had been cordial enough, though. Ushering her into his oak and green leather consulting room, he had listened carefully to her descrip-tion of the Mosier case and the quandary over whether or not Tug was guilty of murder.

"And what do you want me to do, Miss Hill?" he asked when Pow-ell's explanation finally wound down.

"Well, I was wondering if you could examine my client and try to determine whether or not he did it. Give him some tests, perhaps."

Arthur Timmons considered the matter for a few moments. "Tests," he mused. "There are some measures that we could take to try to restore his memory of the night in question. Hypnosis. Using a drug to put him into a semiconscious state so that he can discuss that night without inhibitions. But are you sure you want to do that?"

"Why wouldn't I?" asked A. P. Hill.

"Because he might remember. Right now you can plead your client innocent with perfect sincerity, since you have no conclusive evidence that he did it. But what are you going to do if I regress him, and he promptly confesses to the murder?"

A. P. Hill looked thoughtful. "I suppose I would have to concentrate on mitigating circumstances," she said. "Diminished capacity. Accident. I'd have to know the circumstances before I could make any decision about how to proceed. I think, though, that Tug Mosier would like to go through with the tests, if possible. He's grief-stricken over Misti Hale's death, and he genuinely seems to want to know if he did it."

Dr. Timmons scribbled a few notes and then looked up with a sad smile. "I think you're taking a great risk by doing this," he said. "It has been my experience that most trial lawyers aren't interested in the truth. They're interested in a game plan. But talk to your client, Miss Hill. If he truly wants to resolve the question of his guilt, I will do what I can to assist you."

"There's one other thing," said Powell. "I'm court-appointed, you see, and we don't have any money to spend on medical experts."

"I assumed that," said Timmons, still smiling. "Poor and honest seem to go together, don't they?"

◆   ◆   ◆

EDITH CAME INTO THE OFFICE, closed the door behind her, and stood with her back against it. Her expression brought to mind the expendable blonde in reel one of a horror movie.

"What is it?" chuckled Bill. "Mr. Trowbridge in person?"

Edith shook her head. "It's that ornery man who bought the Home for Confederate Women, and if you thought he was bad before, you ought to see him now. He's about ready to spit nails."

"Oh, boy! I hope it isn't termites. Did he say what he wanted?"

"No, but judging from his expression, I'd say he wants to use your scalp for pom-poms."

"Hmm," said Bill. "That doesn't sound good. Is Powell here? No, of course not. She's in Richmond, isn't she? Well, let them in, and I'll try to straighten this out."

"Okay," said Edith. "I just thought I'd warn you." She mustered a wan smile and went out to face the visitors. Seconds later, Bill's door burst open again, and John Huff stormed in, followed by an officious-looking young man with a clipboard.

"Hello, Mr. Huff," said Bill, coming out from behind his desk with an outstretched hand. "What can I do for you?"

Huff ignored the friendly greeting and turned to his companion. "That's him."

Randolph Custis Byrd bustled forward and introduced himself in condescending tones. "Am I to understand that you sold the Home for Confederate Women to this gentleman last month for more than one million dollars?"

"I represented the sellers," said Bill. "Why? What's the matter?"

"You represented the sellers," echoed Byrd with a tight little smile. "And who *were* the sellers, may one ask?"

"Well . . . the Confederate widows. Daughters, actually, I think. There were eight of them. Miss Dabney, Miss Pendleton . . . I could look up the names."

"I never saw them," said John Huff. "*You* ran the ad in the newspaper."

"Well, yes," Bill admitted. "They instructed me to. They're very elderly, and they didn't want to be bothered with telephone calls."

"And when I flew down to Danville, you drove me out to the house and showed me around, but there was no one else there."

"They went out to tea," stammered Bill. "They were a little upset about . . . uh . . . selling their home."

"But you didn't see them at all, Mr. Huff?" asked Byrd.

"I did not."

"And then you decided to purchase the house," Byrd continued, staring at Bill as he spoke. "You signed the papers here, I believe?"

"That's right," said Huff grimly. "And *he* signed on behalf of the sellers. Said he had their power of attorney. We transferred the money from my bank to an account in *his* name."

Bill's head was reeling, and for a moment he thought he was back in one of his bar exam nightmares. "I can explain all that," he stammered. "The old ladies didn't want to come down to the office because one of them had a doctor's appointment. It was short notice, you remember."

"What doctor?" said Byrd quickly.

"How should I know?" snapped Bill. "I can't even remember which old lady. We could ask them, I suppose. Now, will one of you tell me what this is all about?"

Huff ignored the question. "What did you do with the money, Mac-Pherson?"

Bill blushed. "It's going to sound crazy," he said with a little laugh.

"But the old ladies claimed they didn't trust American banks. They asked me to deposit the money in a numbered account in the Cayman Islands. Can you imagine?"

Nobody laughed with him.

John Huff looked like a thundercloud. "A numbered account in the Cayman Islands! I'm surprised you had enough savvy to come up with that."

"I didn't do it," said Bill. "The old ladies did. I don't know how they came up with the notion."

"Banks in the Cayman Islands won't give out any information about their accounts," said Huff. "They won't say how much money the account holds, and they won't tell you whose account it is, either. Of course you knew that."

Bill looked from Huff to Byrd and back again in disbelief. "You don't think I did it?" he gasped. "You think *I* opened that account and kept the money?"

"It seems obvious to me," said Huff, stone-faced.

"But the fraud goes well beyond that," Byrd pointed out. "That house is state property. We had filed a writ of eminent domain, claiming the property for use as an art museum for southwest Virginia. No one had any authority to sell it."

"We did a title search," Bill protested. "We got a clear title! Mr. Huff's lawyer must have double-checked that."

"I intend to find out," said Huff grimly. "And if he didn't, I'll have his job at Fremont, Shields & Banks!"

"If the acquisition notice is not on file in the courthouse, that adds to the seriousness of the fraud," said Byrd. "Tampering with legal documents for the purpose of fraud."

"But I didn't!" wailed Bill. "At least I didn't do the title search. But Edith wouldn't do a thing like that."

"Get her in here," said Huff.

Edith Creech appeared in the doorway. Huff, his eyes glittering like a snake's, waved the title in front of her, and said, "MacPherson claims that you did this title search. Is that correct?"

"I went to the courthouse and found it," said Edith warily. "Why?"

"Did you leave out anything? A document with a state seal on it, for example?" asked Custis Byrd.

"I don't think so."

"And you witnessed this power of attorney, signed by the eight residents of the Home for Confederate Women."

Edith looked at the paper. Then she looked at Bill. And back at the paper. "Uh . . . well . . ."

"Did you or did you not witness these signatures?"

"What did he say?" Edith hedged.

"It's all right, Edith," sighed Bill. "I'll tell them. I forgot to take Edith with me when I went out to have the paper signed. We had only about twelve hours' notice about the closing, and she was very busy typing up all the documents we needed. By the time I realized that it wasn't notarized, one of the women had gone for the evening, and we had a ton of work to do, so she took my word for it."

"Of course we will be reporting this to the state bar association, as well as to the proper legal authorities," said Byrd in a self-righteous pout.

"Wait," said Bill. "Flora Dabney can clear this up. Just call her and ask her about the bank account and the newspaper ad—and all the rest of it." He reached for the telephone book. "They said they were going to be moving to the Oakmont Nursing Home. They even invited me to come and have tea with them. Ah, here's the number. We'll soon straighten this out."

Bill looked at the ceiling while he listened to the phone ring. What incredible bad luck, he was thinking. Everything going wrong, all on the same case. He'd catch hell for that notary business, and A. P. Hill would be thoroughly pissed about this snafu in the new firm, no matter how brief a mix-up it proved to be. The ringing stopped.

"Hello," said Bill eagerly. "Oakmont Nursing Home? May I speak to Miss Flora Dabney, please? She's a new resident. She and the other former residents of the Home for Confederate Women just moved to your facility—oh, about a week ago . . . What? Are you sure? Could you check? Maybe somebody else? . . . Oh, you do." Bill's voice became progressively muted as the conversation continued. Finally he muttered a lifeless thank-you and hung up.

"I don't understand," he said. "They're not there. The director of Oakmont says that she's never heard of them. Oakmont—I'm sure that's what Flora Dabney said."

"Maybe they changed their minds," Edith suggested. "You know how old ladies are. Try the other retirement communities."

"Did you ever actually see any of these women?" Custis Byrd wanted to know.

"Well . . . no," said Edith after a moment's thought. "But I've heard so much about them. Miss Dabney came by the office on my day off." She turned to Bill. "Was Powell here? Did she meet them?"

Bill shook his head. "I don't know where she was. A meeting, I think. But Miss Dabney sent me a photograph of herself." He reached in the desk drawer and pulled out the sepia portrait of the Edwardian girl.

Huff and Byrd were not impressed. "You can buy a hundred photos like that in any antique shop," said Custis Byrd. "Instant ancestors for a dollar apiece. I'd hardly call that picture evidence."

"Try the other nursing homes," Edith said again. "Miss Dabney can clear all this up in two minutes."

"If there *is* a Miss Dabney," Byrd snickered.

Ten minutes later, Bill had completed four more phone calls, each following the pattern of the first. There were no more retirement communities to try. Then he called directory assistance in search of a telephone listing for Flora Dabney and for each of the other ladies. Nothing.

"But it just doesn't make sense," Bill kept saying. "Where could they be? They couldn't just vanish into thin air!"

John Huff and Custis Byrd looked at each other. Huff stood up. "Well, I think that's all," he said, motioning for Byrd to follow him. "We'll be going now."

"Going?" echoed Bill, standing up as if he wanted to run after them.

"Yes," said Huff. "We'll let the authorities take it from here. You can explain this to the police. And I'm sure they'll want to know what you did with the bodies of the eight defenseless old ladies who lived in the Home. You didn't bury them in the basement, did you?"

◆ ◆ ◆

JIMMY STEWART STOOD UP and embraced the young boy with the crutch. The congregation burst into song as the credits rolled.

The Confederate soldier switched off the video. On the tiny rug that constituted A. P. Hill's living room, two other uniformed men scribbled furiously in spiral notebooks, while on the two sofas more contemporarily dressed gentlemen and A. P. Hill herself were similarly engaged in composition. Aside from sporadic muttering over an answer, no one spoke. Only the whir of the rewinding cassette recorder broke the silence.

Even in a less prosaic setting, no knowledgeable observer would have mistaken the uniformed men for Confederate ghosts. Their gray wool coats were clean and undamaged, and they all wore leather boots. Besides, they were at least ten years too old and forty pounds too heavy to have been the boys who really fought that distant war. These were the sunshine soldiers who fought the war summers and weekends, without grapeshot, dysentery, gangrene, malnutrition, or conspicuous personal inconvenience. They were the reenactors.

Tonight, though, they were not on duty, even in their mythic Confederacy. They were in uniform just for the fun of it, attending a meeting of the local Civil War Roundtable Discussion Group, which was assembled at the home of A. P. Hill, descendant and namesake of the general. The evening's entertainment had been a showing of *Shenandoah*, a Civil War–set film of the 1960s starring James Stewart. It was a sad and stirring saga of the war in Virginia, but in this audience wet handkerchiefs were conspicuously absent.

A. P. Hill went to the kitchen and brought back coffee and plates of cake and cookies. When the rations had been distributed to the troops, she said, "All right, is everybody ready? Put your pens on the table now, so no one can be accused of modifying his comments. Who wants to go first?"

An elderly man in a black suit raised his hand. "I got eight," he announced. "Shall I read them out?"

"Go on, Dr. Howe. The rest of us will check off any of our responses that duplicate yours."

"First, the scenery was wrong. Does that count? It certainly was not Virginia."

"They filmed it in Oregon," said Powell Hill. "I don't think we can fault them for that, though. Movies almost never get produced in a logical setting. Go on to the next one."

"According to the film, the year was 1864, and Jimmy Stewart still had six grown sons living at home on his farm in the middle of a war zone. No way. The Confederacy introduced conscription in 1861. Those boys would *all* have been drafted. So would their dad, more than likely."

Everyone in the room nodded. Most retrieved their pens and made check marks on their note pads.

"It *might* have worked if you'd changed the location," Ken Filban suggested. He was a bank executive from East Tennessee. "According to the movie, they were on a five-hundred-acre farm near Harrisonburg."

"Which should have been crawling with hired help," said Confederate corporal Scott Chambers, otherwise a driver for UPS. "In the days before mechanized farming, you couldn't cultivate five hundred acres with five men and two young women to run the house. They weren't ranchers; they were farmers."

"Like I said, change the location and it might have been plausible," Ken Filban said. "Make the Anderson farm a fifty-acre place tucked into a hollow in the North Carolina or Tennessee mountains, and chances are they could have got away with ignoring the war. Family legend had it that all my great-great-uncles spent the war dodging both armies—and never served a day."

Dr. Howe cleared his throat. "It's still my turn. Number two: the rifles were wrong." Unanimous check marks.

"They even got the rifles wrong in *Glory*," said A. P. Hill. "They had the soldiers checking serial numbers. It was more accurate than this movie, though."

"Number three: they had a black Union soldier serving in a white regiment. That didn't happen."

"How about when Jimmy Stewart's family stopped the Union train and the Federals didn't shoot them? Six guys stopping a train! And what did the Federals have, five guys guarding a couple of hundred prisoners on that train?" Ken Filban was laughing at the naïveté of moviemakers.

Powell Hill shrugged. "That's Hollywood. Still, the film had some good qualities. The main characters were Southerners who weren't made to sound like idiots. And the rural people weren't portrayed as hicks."

"It seemed like a Western to me. Didn't it look like a Western to you?"

"The director's next job was the television series *Bonanza*," said Dr. Howe.

"Yeah, but maybe that wasn't inaccurate," said Scott Chambers thoughtfully. "Only thirty years earlier, some of Virginia was Indian country. I think we *were* the West in those days."

"Costumes!" said Dr. Howe, still trying to finish his list. "It was 1864 and we were seeing Confederate soldiers who weren't in rags. And they had shoes."

"Everybody was too well dressed," Powell agreed. "After four years of war, even the civilians should have been thin and shabby, wearing mended old clothes."

"Well, that covers my list!" said the history professor, crossing off the last objection on his pad. "That was fun. What shall we do next? *Gone With the Wind*?"

A. P. Hill shook her head. "None of us can write that fast," she said.

"Those Hollywood people should try reenacting," said Ken Filban. "You learn a lot about war from tramping around in the heat in a wool outfit loaded down with heavy equipment."

Scott Chambers nodded. "It's a funny feeling, walking in a straight line toward a bunch of guys holding bayonets. Even when you know they're acting."

"Same time next week?" asked Dr. Howe. "My place."

"I won't be able to come," said A. P. Hill. "I have a trial coming up out of town, starting Monday."

"Will you be—" Ken Filban glanced apprehensively at the elderly Dr. Howe. "Will you be coming out this weekend?"

Confederate corporal A. P. Hill gave him a trace of a smile. They were careful not to talk about her reenactment activities in front of any possible Silverbacks. "See you there," she said.

◆   ◆   ◆

"I'll tie back my hair; men's clothing I'll put on,
        And I'll pass as your comrade as we march along.
I'll pass as your comrade. No one will ever know . . .
        Won't you let me go with you?"—"No, my love, no."
                                                —"The Cruel War"

A. P. HILL PARKED HER CAR in the out-of-the-way lot
reserved for those taking part in the battle and made her way along the
dirt path to the place of assembly. She was already in full regalia for the
day's event: hair tucked under her kepi cap, rimless glasses in place, and
her uniform and brogans carefully adjusted to envelop her in anonym-
ity. She looked like a very young Confederate soldier—one of the most
authentic looking present because of her small stature and slender

build. She sometimes wondered at the illogic of the men who controlled the hobby, who frowned upon any woman taking part, but would happily open their ranks to 250-pound men in their fifties. Accuracy, she decided, was a state of mind.

It was just past nine o'clock, and already the sun was blazing. There would be people passing out today in their wool uniforms. It was a day that you could smell the enemy from across the field. Some of the purists refused to have their uniforms cleaned *ever*, which was all very accurate, but it was hard on their fellow soldiers. Powell was careful to keep her uniform believably dirty, but she drew the line at actual stench.

Today's reenactment was a large, staged battle on land that was now a national park in Virginia. The park service had seen to it that the event was well publicized, so the reenactors could expect a substantial crowd to turn up to observe the battle. That was not particularly anachronistic, either, she reflected. During the real war, at the first battle of Bull Run, sightseers from Washington had driven out to the battlefield in buckboards to picnic on the hillsides and watch the confrontation. The afternoon hadn't quite gone as planned, though, and the spectators soon found themselves caught in the congestion of a retreating Union army, stampeding back to Washington, while the Confederate generals pleaded with President Davis to let them follow and seize the enemy's capital.

What if they had?

Historians had toyed with that riddle for a hundred years and more. Powell herself had argued the point more than once at meetings of the Civil War Roundtable. What difference would it have made? In the long run—not much, in the opinion of A. P. Hill. Slavery was already a dying institution, thanks to new philosophies of humanitarianism and technological advancements like the cotton gin. The practice had died out in South America in the 1880s without a civil war to enforce the measure, and she thought that something similar might have happened in the Confederacy, if it had survived. Slavery would have been legislated out of existence in the South, just as the North had finally put an end to its own form of slavery: the urban sweatshops that imprisoned child workers and paid the poor pennies a day for sixteen hours of toil. The two countries would have existed separately for a while—maybe even for half a century—but she had always argued that before World

War I, the two halves of the union would have come together again. After all, they would not have the bitterness that characterized sectional feeling even to this day. The two nations would have reunited for economic and political reasons. Or failing that, they would cooperate in much the same way that the United States now works with Canada, without exhibiting any particular inclination to march in and claim the northern territories for annexation.

She put away all thoughts of an alternate political future for the South. Today it was 1862, and Stonewall Jackson was going to win the battle in precisely the historical way, just as he must go on to lose the war in the foreseeable future. Now it was time to forget about the twentieth century. A. P. Hill felt that reenacting should be mental as well as physical. She tried to banish concerns about Tug Mosier's trial and all the nagging reminders of modern existence as she concentrated on the field and the coming battle and the identity of a southwest Virginia corporal known to his unit as Andy Hill.

She was about to go in search of Ken Filban when she passed a small brick building that reminded her of one small twentieth-century convenience that she needed to avail herself of before she slipped away into the past. Squatting in the weeds without toilet paper was no fun. She decided to solve the problem before she went off to battle. Besides, she could use one last look in a mirror to check her appearance.

Three minutes later, with her hat newly adjusted and her face scrubbed clean of all lingering lipstick traces, Powell Hill emerged from the ladies' rest room to find her way blocked by a burly man in a National Park Service uniform.

He glowered at her as if she were a potato bug, looking at the sign marked LADIES and giving her a long once-over from cap to brogans. "What were you doing in there?"

A. P. Hill scowled back. "What do you think?"

The man rocked back on his heels with a satisfied expression that was a thousand miles from kindness. "If you brought your regular clothes, you can stay and watch the battle, little lady," he said with a smirk. "Otherwise, you can go on back to your car and leave the park. You won't be playing soldier today."

Against her better judgment, Powell decided to reason with him. "Look," she said, "if you hadn't caught me coming out of the ladies' room, you would never have known that I'm female. Spectators fifty yards away sure can't tell it, and my gear is a hundred percent authentic. I've been doing this for a couple of years now. What's the harm in letting me take part?"

"I'm not going to argue with you," said the park official. "I'm taking you back to your car."

"You're violating my civil rights," said A. P. Hill with a mulish look in her eyes.

"We want an authentic reenactment, miss. And women soldiers aren't accurate."

"The hell they aren't!" she said, a good deal more loudly than diplomacy would dictate. "That shows how damn little you know about the war! Have you ever heard of Sarah Edmonds Seelye? She fought in the Second Michigan Infantry under the name of Franklin Thompson! And so-called Albert Cashier of the 95th Illinois was female. So were about four hundred other women who disguised themselves as men and fought. At least one was killed at Antietam!"

"Reenactments are supposed to portray the norm," said the man with a stony gaze. "Women soldiers were not the norm. Now take off the uniform or leave."

"But there *were* female soldiers!"

"Not in my park. Now get going before I have you arrested for trespassing."

An expression of holy joy lingered on Powell Hill's face for a moment as she looked up at him, but then she remembered Tug Mosier's trial, and she realized that she couldn't indulge herself to fight this moron. With a look of utter defeat that was not entirely sincere, A. P. Hill allowed herself to be marched summarily back to her car. Before she drove away, she made a note of the park ranger's name and description.

Edinburgh
In haste

Dear Bill,

I am taking the next plane over. Arriving Dulles via British Airways; Danville by puddlejumper. Don't bother to meet me.

Elizabeth

"War is hell."
—GENERAL WILLIAM TECUMSEH SHERMAN

CHAPTER

7

''D O Y O U H A V E A N Y T H I N G to declare?" the customs man asked me as I shuffled past him with my one old suitcase.

"Yes," I said, stifling a yawn. "It's past midnight."

He consulted his watch. "Seven-fifteen, ma'am."

"Not according to my body," I told him wearily. Easy for him to proclaim this the shank of the evening. *He* hadn't climbed aboard a plane in Scotland at two in the afternoon and winged his way across the

Atlantic in a seat the size of a panty-hose egg to arrive hot and thirsty ten hours later, in what my body damn well knows is the middle of the night, only to have twenty minutes to hustle through customs to make my flight connection: an airborne Dixie Cup bound for sleepy little Danville. Things had been pretty peaceful in rural Virginia since the Late Unpleasantness in 1865, but my family seemed determined to make up for more than a century of uneventfulness.

I ignored the whole situation for as long as I could. When Mother wrote me a cheery little letter bomb announcing that she and my father were thinking of "going their separate ways" (after nearly thirty years!), I hoped for the best, but decided that I should stay out of it, assuming that they could resolve their differences on their own. Surely, I thought, with a decades-old relationship at stake, they won't do anything hasty. When I heard from my brother that Dad had a girlfriend (who is probably named Bambi, and whose IQ probably equals her bust size), I will admit that I became somewhat more concerned about the situation, but I coped. (No matter what my husband says, I feel that throwing chairs is an excellent way of channeling stress into physical exertion; the incident had nothing whatever to do with feelings of rage or frustration.) Which reminds me that while I am over here, I must see if the Thomasville Gallery is having anything in the way of a sale on new dining room chairs. Perhaps in oak, which has a reputation for being a very sturdy wood. Cameron can say what he likes, but throwing things is a better reaction to stress than eating, which is temporarily comforting, but only creates more stress in the long run, when one begins to break chairs simply by *sitting* in them.

Despite the strain I remained firm in my resolve to stay out of the family crisis. Even Bambi or whatever her name is could not induce me to cross the Atlantic, leaving home and husband, though. Least said, soonest mended, they say. But I did check to make sure that my passport was up-to-date and that my luggage tags had the correct address in Edinburgh. Just as well that I did, because yesterday my brother contacted me with the news that he is suspected of mass murder and accused of stealing a fortune. That was too much.

I decided that I'd better fly home before my demented relatives decided to take over an air force base and start the War all over again. Even Cameron had to admit that things seemed out of hand with the stateside branch of the family; so he didn't try to talk me out of going.

But he couldn't take time off to come with me. I suppose it's just as well that I haven't yet found a job in Scotland; there was no telling how long I was going to have to stay in Virginia. With a funeral, you just attend, settle matters concerning the estate if you must, and then return to your regular life, but no one in my family had the decorum to *die*. I suppose I'll feel very guilty for making that wisecrack, but I'm angry now—and my family is being particularly exasperating. They're probably doing this just to drive me crazy and get the inheritance.

I took the new scandalous royal biography with me on the plane for reading matter. It was comforting to be reminded that no family is immune from turmoil, but even the tale of a princess's drinking problem couldn't hold my attention. I kept thinking of Aunt Amanda's reaction to my parents' breakup, assuming that anybody had been fool enough to tell her. "I knew it wouldn't last," she'd sniff. "They eloped."

And then I'd think about poor old Bill, who seemed to have drifted into law school because a college degree wasn't enough anymore for ambitious middle-class parents. It wasn't enough for the modern job market, either. Fast-food restaurant managers had college degrees these days; everybody else needed an extra piece of paper to move upward.

I remember my brother, Bill, as a towheaded kid captivated by magic acts on television. He'd use his allowance to buy simple tricks, and then he'd inflict them on the family and the Scout troop at the slightest lull in conversation. Our enthusiasm hadn't been exactly unbounded, and after a few years of saying, "Pick a card, any card," to the backs of a stampeding audience, he gave it up and retreated into his schoolwork. He'd graduated Phi Beta Kappa from William and Mary, and had been accepted into law school without much difficulty. But I never saw him talk about law school with anything like the glow he used to have for his hokey magic tricks. Sometimes I wondered if his interminable stay in law school had been a postponement of his inevitable humdrum fate. That made me sad. For all the teasing I go through for my career (*grave-robbing*, as my cousin Geoffrey puts it), I genuinely enjoyed forensic anthropology, solving death's little puzzles based on the clues left behind in the human body. I wished that I could be sure that Bill was as happy in his expensively acquired profession.

One thing I was sure of, though: Bill MacPherson was not a crook. And there was absolutely no way that he could be a murderer. Even as a kid, he'd been a halfhearted squabbler, generally losing the last piece of cake or the new toy to me not because he was unselfish, but because he didn't really care enough to make a fuss about things. I couldn't imagine him beset with any of the aggressive sins, like avarice or larceny. I could, however, envision his being careless in detail or overly trusting of other people (when we were kids, he used to let *me* divide up the ice cream), but there is no way that my brother could have done what he stands accused of. No way.

"Give me something with an air bag," I told the car-rental people at the Danville airport. I'd been driving in Scotland for so long that I didn't trust myself to make an uneventful transition back to the right side of the road, especially when I had so many other things to worry about.

Bill would have picked me up at the airport, but I didn't want to be dependent on him for transportation. I didn't know Danville very well, but a city map came with the car, and Danville isn't large enough to get lost in. It's the kind of place where people read the newspaper to see who has been caught. I knew that my brother's office and his apartment were in the same downtown building, so the chances of finding him at this hour seemed excellent. I wasn't ready to go to my parents' house yet. The thought gave me chills.

I crossed the Dan River on the old bridge that led downtown and found a parking place just outside the law office building. The street was deserted and the sky had a haze of reflected light from the city, hiding the stars. I wondered if I should have picked up a pizza on my way in. When he's worried, Bill forgets to eat. I never have that problem.

I hurried up the stairs, knowing that if I stopped to think about what to say, I might turn around and run. The door to the office was closed, but the light was on. I looked at the frosted glass, emblazoned with the names MacPherson and Hill, wishing I'd come to visit in time to be proud of his achievement.

He was sitting in his office, head in his hands, oblivious to the sound of the door opening and my footsteps in the outer office. I slipped in quietly and sat down in the chair beside his desk. "I just happened to be in the neighborhood," I said softly. "Thought I'd stop in."

Bill looked up and tried to muster a smile, but he looked like a tired old horse. "Hello, Elizabeth. If you've come to take me home with you, don't bother. I think we have an extradition agreement with Scotland."

"How about Beirut?" I said, smiling back. "It would seem peaceful after your experiences here. Anyhow, I didn't come to help you escape, but I could buy you dinner. Then we could talk about getting you a lawyer."

Bill shrugged. "I *am* a lawyer. And I don't think much of my case. As for dinner, I don't seem to be hungry these days, either."

"Is it as serious as you made it sound in your telegram? I mean, has anything changed?"

"No. The old ladies are gone, the money is still missing, and the Commonwealth of Virginia is still insisting that they had issued an order of eminent domain, claiming the property for the state. That about covers it, I think. Suspicion of murder, embezzlement, fraud. At least it hasn't hit the papers yet. They've given me a couple of days to try to straighten things out—probably because I'm a lawyer. Even a lowly one apparently has some rank. But when the case goes to the grand jury, they'll go public, and then I'm finished."

I glanced around his Goodwill-furnished office and saw what looked to be a stuffed groundhog in a black robe standing on a small table. "Have you thought about pleading insanity?" I asked.

Bill made a face at me. "Since when do you object to having dead things around the office?"

"I draw the line at dressing them up," I told him. "He is kind of cute, though." I was thinking how much fun it would be to hide him in Cousin Geoffrey's bed.

"His name is Flea Bailey," said Bill. "You can take care of him when I go to the slammer."

"That won't happen. Thanks to our late great-aunt Augusta, I have money, remember? We'll hire you the best lawyer in the state."

Bill shook his head. "That's just what I don't want. Don't you see? If any of the *real* lawyers around here find out how badly I've screwed up, I'll never get into a decent firm! My only hope is to get out of this on my own before anybody finds out."

I had never seen him this depressed. Not even when he was failing calculus. "What does your law partner say about all this?" I asked.

"I didn't tell her," he sighed. "She's out of town, defending her first client in a murder trial. She doesn't need to be worrying about me. I keep hoping I'll get it straightened out before it's necessary to tell her."

"I was hoping to meet her," I said. Intelligent women in the vicinity of my brother are a novelty. "Well, maybe later. I plan to be around for a while. I want to hear exactly what happened with this real estate transaction that went sour. But could you tell me on the way to a restaurant?"

By the time he finished the story of the Confederate women in all its intricate and puzzling detail, I was pouring Sweet'n Low into my fourth glass of iced tea. I missed iced tea in Scotland. I missed ice. Now, though, I was barely tasting the tea, so engrossed had I been in my brother's account of the house sale. He had eaten most of a cheeseburger, and now he was pushing French fries around on his plate while he described the visit from John Huff and the assistant state director of art and antiquities.

"I thought I was doing those old dears a favor," he mumbled.

"You would," I told him. "It's all that vestigial Southern chivalry in your veins. You think that old ladies are sweet and helpless, and that you are doing them a kindness by offering them the assistance of your competent little old self."

"But why would they want to get me in trouble?" moaned Bill. "They were so nice. Look, one of them even gave me a Confederate penny as a souvenir of my first case." He pulled the shiny copper coin out of his pocket and held it up so that I could see.

"Maybe that's what they thought your services were worth," I said, and instantly regretted it, because Bill got that hurt look that always used to make me give him back the last cookie. "I'm sorry I said that," I mumbled.

"I tried to do it right," he said sadly. "And I didn't do anything to make them mad at me. I'm too insignificant to have enemies."

"I expect you are, Bill. I don't think you were the target at all. I think they just needed a lawyer. If you'll pardon my saying so, they probably wanted the dumbest lawyer they could find."

Bill groaned. "They chose well. Fresh out of law school, wet behind the ears. I was the perfect fool all right. I suppose the real scam was selling the house before the state could evict them?"

"That seems likely." I yawned again. Three A.M. Edinburgh time.

Bill glanced at his watch. "You must be comatose by now, kid. Where are you staying? With Mom?"

"Not if I can help it," I said quickly. "How are things going with them, anyway?"

"If I had time to worry about them, I would. They won't talk to each other, and neither of them seems anxious to confide in me, either. Maybe you'll have better luck."

"Do they know about the trouble you're in?"

He shook his head. "They're not too much fun to have around right now, so I thought I'd try to get out of it on my own. Otherwise there might be a reverse custody battle of sorts: both of them fighting to see who has to claim me."

"But you told me about it."

"Oh, *you*," said my brother. "What do you care? Trouble is your middle name. I thought you might actually enjoy it."

"I wouldn't go that far," I said, finishing off the last of my tea. "But I don't intend to sit by and watch it happen. I think I'll find the old ladies and see what they have to say."

"I've tried," said Bill. "They aren't in the retirement community they said they were going to. I can't find them anywhere."

"How long have we got?"

"Before the grand jury? About ten days."

"I'll find them," I told him. I should have commended Bill on his customary competence and said I'd just search for the old ladies because I had so much free time and because I might get lucky; but I was too jet-lagged for conversational acrobatics. Southern women spend a lifetime playing down their abilities as a form of politeness. I've done it all my life, but I didn't have time for charades at that moment. I had only ten days to find eight old ladies who were also Southern and—Bill's opinion notwithstanding—probably smarter than I was.

◆   ◆   ◆

A. P. HILL TOOK ANOTHER SIP of cold coffee, and looked appraisingly at her client. He was paler now, after a few weeks in prison, but his white T-shirt still bulged with pasty fat. Apparently, he hadn't found jail food inedible, but the fare wasn't doing much for his health. His shaggy hair was now greasy and in need of cutting, and his chin was blue with beard stubble. Powell wished he looked more appealing; juries had qualms about convicting good-looking people. They'd put Tug Mosier away without batting an eye. He looked like the villain on a TV movie of the week.

"Are you sure you want to do this, Tug?"

He blinked at her as though it were a trick question. She was the first authority figure who had ever been on his side, and he couldn't quite separate her from the bullying schoolteachers and pitiless bureaucrats who peopled his past. Sometimes he thought he might trust her, but even if she meant well, she might be too innocent and powerless to do him any good against the System. "Well, I reckon I ought to find out for sure one way or the other." He hesitated. "But if it's bad—what we find out—can we just keep it to ourselves?"

"If it's bad, neither you nor Dr. Timmons will be called upon to testify," Powell promised him. "But in case it isn't, we're going to make a tape of the session. Okay?"

"I guess y'all know best," he said, shifting his manacled hands and giving them a wary smile. Tug Mosier didn't trust anybody who'd admit to having gone to college. In the fat cats' world he was a barn rat, and it was always open season.

Dr. Timmons ushered the uniformed guard to the door of the treatment room. "You'll have to wait outside," he said. "The room isn't soundproof. You won't be able to hear the session, but if there's any disturbance, it will come through the walls, and you may interrupt. Don't expect any trouble, though. I'm going to sedate him right away."

The guard looked suspiciously at Tug Mosier's hulking form. "I'm right outside," he said.

They had borrowed a room at the county hospital, and set up an evening session so as not to interfere with the normal routine of the clinic. It was a small windowless room, containing only a bare metal desk and three straight-backed metal chairs. On the desk, they had placed Powell Hill's tape recorder, a yellow legal pad, and Timmons's medical supplies. Dr. Timmons made his preparations, talking in a low reassuring voice to the manacled patient. "This won't hurt, Mr. Mosier. It may not even work. But if it does, you'll remember the night in question as if it were a movie that you were watching on television. Do you understand?"

Tug Mosier shrugged. "I know how to watch television, if that's what you mean, doc."

"That's about all there is to it. When I put you under, you watch that movie screen in your head, and when I ask you to, you describe for us the things that you see taking place. It's easy. Can you do that?"

"I reckon." People had been telling Tug Mosier how easy things were all his life. Making passing grades, holding down a job, staying sober. But nothing came easy to him.

Timmons filled the hypodermic needle and held it up for his inspection. "Seven and a half grains of sodium amytal," he said. "This ought to help you to remember. You'll feel the pinprick of the needle, but that's all. Are you ready?"

Tug Mosier glanced at his attorney, who nodded almost imperceptibly. He held out his arm. "Go on and stick me, then."

While they waited for the drug to take effect, Powell Hill thought about the forthcoming trial. She wondered if she had insisted on this psychological evaluation for Tug Mosier's sake, or for her own peace of mind. She was just beginning her career in law. She still wanted to know if things were true or false. Later, she'd heard, it all turned into a complex chess game. And only the skill of the moves mattered any longer.

"He's ready," said Timmons softly.

Tug Mosier seemed awake, but more subdued than before. He sat slack-jawed in his steel-frame chair, staring at the lime-green wall with a furrowed expression of concentration.

"Can you hear me, Tug?"

"Yeah." The reply was a voiceless whisper.

"We're going back to the last time you saw Misti. I want you to watch yourself on that wall there. That's where the movie's showing. Do you see yourself out drinking with the boys?"

"Yeah."

"You see it happening, Tug, but you won't feel it this time. You're not going to get high just from watching, understand?"

Tug's head jerked in what might have been a yes. He was still staring at the lime-colored wall, almost oblivious to their presence.

"Tell me when you see yourself leaving the party, Tug. Can you fast-forward to that part now?"

"Okay. Getting my jacket on. Heading for the door."

"You're drunk, though, in the movie, aren't you? Not walking very well?"

"S'right."

"Does the gang say goodbye to you?"

"Naw. Too busy partying. Nobody gives a—"

"Does anybody go with you? Maybe you needed some help getting home."

"Yeah. Somebody's holding on to me."

Timmons and Powell Hill looked at each other. After a moment of silence, the doctor went on in a carefully offhand tone. "Can you see who it is, Tug?"

"Yeah. Red. Red Dowdy?"

Powell Hill scribbled the name on the note pad and waited with pencil poised for her client to continue. "Get a description," she mouthed silently to Timmons.

"What does Red Dowdy look like, Tug?" asked Timmons with casual interest.

"Tall drink of water. Stringy red hair. Gap-toothed. Boots."

"And have you reached your car yet, Tug?"

"Yeah. Sitting in it. Head's spinning too much to drive."

"Did Dowdy get in the car, too?"

"He's pushing me over. Thinks he can drive better."

"Do you let him?"

"Yeah. Too dizzy to argue."

"What happens next, Tug?"

"He's shaking me. We're in the driveway of the house."

"Your house? The place where Misti Lynn is waiting?"

"Yeah. He's pushing me out of the car. I feel like I'm gonna be sick."

"But you go inside. Does Red go in with you?"

Tug Mosier's eyes widened as he stared at the pale green wall, watching Misti Lynn Hale die again.

◆　◆　◆

JOHN HUFF KNEW that soon he would have to return to his business up north, but before he left, he intended to have matters well under way for a prosecution in the case of his house purchase. He didn't suppose that MacPherson would get anything really satisfying, like the death penalty, even in a blood-and-guts state like Virginia. Even so, Huff was determined to see that the local authorities prosecuted the matter to the fullest possible extent. No one made a fool of John Huff and escaped unscathed.

He was in the back parlor of the Home for Confederate Women, still fully clothed although it was well past midnight. A full moon shone through the uncurtained window, giving the room an air of romance, but Huff cared nothing for such sentimental twaddle. His attention was centered on the built-in oak bookshelf that stretched from floor to ceiling on either side of the marble fireplace. As he had stipulated, the old ladies had left behind the books—and a sorry lot they generally were, too. He didn't suppose he could get a quarter apiece for most of them at a yard sale. They were a saccharine collection of book-club novels and cheap editions of second-rate poets and historians. Still, he had to examine all of them carefully. He didn't have much time. Soon the state might succeed in getting its house back and he would be forced to leave. But the process would take a little time.

Meanwhile, he had bullied Custis Byrd and his bureaucracy into letting him stay on in the mansion until matters were resolved. Another title search had been initiated immediately after the MacPherson fiasco came to light, and sure enough, there had been no paperwork filed with the deed indicating that the state intended to claim the house. Of course, that didn't let MacPherson off the hook. In fact it got him in deeper, because Byrd was swearing up and down that the kid lawyer had destroyed the evidence of the state's claim. But Huff was quick to point out that *he* had purchased the house in good faith, and that until the state could prove otherwise, the transaction looked legal. *If* they wanted the house, they would have to pay him purchase price plus ten percent. Moreover, he said, he intended to stay in his newly purchased house until somebody gave him his money back. He didn't care who, or how long it took. That sent Byrd flitting away, mumbling to himself about consulting the attorney general, but John Huff didn't care. He would let Fremont, Shields & Banks take care of that. Not, incidentally, Nathan Kimball, who was a reasonably competent errand boy, but not the legal chain saw Huff required for this sort of contretemps.

For now Huff was marginally content. He had possession of the house, and he intended to take full advantage of the situation, even if it meant getting by on very little sleep. It was nearly two A.M. now and he was still stirring. He had searched most of the house by now, but not as thoroughly as he intended to in the days to come. He even planned to rip out the plaster walls if necessary. Failing that, he'd go over the grounds with a metal detector. If he thought he stood a reasonable chance of getting to keep the house, he would have been considerably more careful about the property, but since the state seemed likely to step in and confiscate it at any moment, he decided that he had nothing to lose by taking drastic measures.

After all, the house had a very interesting and complex history. When the word *Danville* caught his eye in the newspaper ad, he began to investigate a hunch. Since then he had studied the house's past in detail. He would have liked an opportunity to take a crowbar to the Summerlin House as well, but that was now a well-guarded local museum, so he had to pin his hopes on the Phillips house and pray that the temporary occupancy of Micajah Clark in April 1865 meant what he thought it did: several million dollars in Confederate gold concealed somewhere on the premises. If he could spirit that out of the state, he didn't care who ended up with the house itself. If he still wanted to become a Virginia gentleman, he could build a dozen such houses with that kind of booty. John Huff's hobby was treasure-hunting.

◆ ◆ ◆

"They couldn't hit an elephant at this dist—"
—LAST WORDS OF
UNION MAJOR SEDGWICK,
WHO WAS MISTAKEN

BETWEEN ATLANTA AND THE SEA . . .

AT HER ADVANCED AGE Flora Dabney felt that she was really too old to command an expedition of this sort, but there didn't seem to be much choice in the matter. The state had forced them out of their rightful home—and really, what could you expect of those carpetbagging Northern Virginians? Not really Southern at all. So now they were fugitives. But Robert E. Lee had lost his citizenship, too. She kept reminding the others that it wasn't what the government thought of you that mattered; it was whether you fought with honor for your Cause.

In truth, their exile wasn't too onerous. Not like poor President Davis's incarceration at Fortress Monroe in Virginia, with leg irons and all. Mary Lee Pendleton had managed to get some of the money from the house sale wired back from the Cayman Islands, whereupon they had purchased a nice large car—and fled. Flora suspected that they might have been able to get a better price on the Chrysler if they hadn't arrived at the Lynchburg dealer's showroom by taxi, but they had decided that haste was worth the few thousand extra they'd paid.

Of course, all eight of them wouldn't fit into anything the dealer had to offer, but that was all right, because Jenny Wade Allan and Julia Hotchkiss weren't in any condition to ride in a getaway car. After the taxi dropped them off at the car dealer, it had sped away again, taking Jenny and Julia to the Roanoke airport, with Anna Douglas along to look after them. (It was fortunate that the taxi driver had agreed to a daily rate, or else they'd have owed him a king's ransom.) Anna had some of the money, and instructions to hire a car and go on ahead to their destination. She had also taken Beauregard, the Home's Confederate cat, in a mesh pet carrier, to be checked on board as "living luggage." The separation had been Dolly Smith's idea. She had insisted that the group split up to travel so that they would be more difficult to trace. All those years of watching gangster movies on *The Late Show* had stood her in good stead as a budding fugitive.

With the two invalids and Anna safely sent away to plague USAir, the remaining five rebels purchased an automobile, paid in cash, and departed before the dealer had time to consider the peculiarity of it all. (He was heard to mutter several times that afternoon, "But they *couldn't* be drug dealers!")

Thank heaven Flora's eyesight was still good, and there weren't any gears to shift anymore in these newfangled cars. She'd never quite gotten the hang of that. But she was a better driver than Ellen Morrison, who tended to get flustered in traffic. Flora did most of the driving, but on interstates, she'd let Ellen take a turn at the wheel. Timid Ellen would pull cautiously into the slow lane and putt along at a painstaking forty-five miles an hour while more daring motorists blitzed past them, sneering. Ellen would flash them an apologetic smile and cautiously accelerate to forty-seven for a mile or two.

At that rate, it had taken them a good deal longer to get to Georgia than might be inferred from a road map of the southeastern states, but when there were no trucks to intimidate them, the drive had been pleasant enough. Dolly had kept up a running commentary on the landscaping of the various homes they passed. She did not approve of potted geraniums as an alternative to hard work in one's garden.

Flora, Lydia, and Mary Lee had spent many hours arguing over their best course of action. Flora wanted to go directly to the rendezvous point in case Anna should have trouble coping with the invalids, Jenny and Julia, but Lydia and Mary Lee were enjoying their first outing in years, and they insisted on sightseeing along the way. Finally Flora gave in and agreed to a few stops: the outlet mall south of Charlotte; some antique shop in Columbia, South Carolina; and a night at Unicoi State Park near Helen, Georgia. (Mary Lee *would* pick up every advertising brochure in the rack at the interstate rest stops!) Flora suspected that there were more direct ways to reach their destination, but since her eyes couldn't manage the fine print on the map, she had to accept Lydia's suggestions for the best routes.

She'd finally balked at Mary Lee's request to see Stone Mountain. "It's south of *Atlanta!*" Flora said, accidentally pressing the horn in her agitation. "You can't tell me *that's* on the way to anywhere!"

"Well, not exactly," Mary Lee admitted. "But I have always wanted to see it. I remember when they dedicated the mountain back in 1925. My father went along for the dedication and brought back one of the commemorative half-dollars made to honor the occasion." She held up the silver coin, which had been set into a ring of silver and made into a necklace. On the shiny face of the U.S. half-dollar were the images of Robert E. Lee and Stonewall Jackson side by side on horseback, and above them a semicircle of stars.

"I wonder how many of those half-dollars the government minted," mused Dolly. "And isn't it amazing that they did it at all? Strike a coin commemorating an old enemy, I mean."

"I've always wanted to see the carvings of the Confederacy on Stone Mountain," said Lydia Bridgeford. "You know, my dear father was a prominent naval officer during the War Between the States."

"So you keep telling us," murmured Mary Lee.

"But it *isn't* on our route," Flora said.

"Let's put it to a vote," said Dolly.

Afterward, Ellen Morrison said that she hadn't liked to disappoint poor Lydia and Mary Lee, which is why she had cast the tie-breaking vote in favor of the detour. Flora continued to grumble about the mutiny, but she grudgingly followed her navigator's directions until they could see the bare stone mountain gleaming on the horizon. It rose up out of the flat Georgia plain like a natural skyscraper, solitary and splendid. "We can stay an hour," Flora warned them. "Then we have to head east again."

Even that had been too long, she decided later. Trust Mary Lee to strike up a conversation with some nice-looking young man in the parking lot, and before you could say "Chickamauga," she was telling him that they were from Danville and they were playing "Do you know so-and-so?" Flora came upon them in the middle of this conversation, and to her horror she discovered that they did seem to have a common acquaintance. They were nodding and smiling to a degree that gave her palpitations. And of course he asked where they were going, at which point Flora gave Mary Lee a sharp jab in the ribs, so she amended her answer to "an island to see our friend Major Edward Anderson." Mary Lee was a dreadful liar. She couldn't even make up a name without accidentally quoting something she'd read.

"Loose lips sink ships!" Flora had hissed at Mary Lee as she hustled her off to the Chrysler. "Do you want to end up in an old folks' home back in Danville?"

"But I didn't tell him who we are," Mary Lee protested, trying to look sweet and helpless.

"Just as well I got to you in time," snapped Flora. "You were about to exchange visiting cards with that whippersnapper. How do you know he's not a policeman?"

"Oh, no, dear. He told me that he's an actor."

"So was John Wilkes Booth," muttered Flora.

"Perhaps we should move along," said Dolly as the rest of them climbed into the car. "I'll feel much better when we've found the gold. Won't you, Flora?"

"If we find it," muttered Flora.

"While we were marching through Georgia"
—SONG COMMEMORATING
SHERMAN'S MARCH

CHAPTER

8

MY BROTHER'S OFFICE is too small to accommodate visitors except on the most temporary basis, but since I needed access to a telephone, it seemed like a logical place from which to work. Bill did not seem to agree, even though I assured him that I would be completely unobtrusive and that he would soon forget my proximity, except when the phone was for me. Men are such territorial creatures; you would have thought there was another rooster on his dunghill the way he glowered at me, rattled his papers, and displayed exaggerated symptoms of claustrophobia.

Finally I pointed to the cloaked rodent on the bookcase. "Anyone who would consent to share an office with *that*," I said, "has absolutely no business objecting to the presence of a charming relative who is merely trying to help."

"I feel like I'm under house arrest," muttered Bill, throwing open the window to let in a blast of steam from a Danville summer afternoon. "Why don't you use A. P. Hill's office? Or Edith's desk? It's her day off."

"I'm a Ph.D.," I reminded him. "I'm not going to masquerade as your receptionist. And as for using your partner's office, I wouldn't dream of intruding into her space because I haven't met her," I said in a voice of sweet reason. "Besides, *she* doesn't need my help. You do."

"You're supposed to be finding the old ladies," Bill replied. "And they're not in here."

The phone rang at that moment, forestalling my next remark, which would have been to explain that I was in the process of tracking the absconding Confederate women, but like any sensible person with management experience, I had delegated the task. First I went to all the local travel agents to see if any of them had assisted in the travel plans of eight elderly women. The initial answer had been negative, but they all agreed to check their records and get back to me. I had told them a pretty story about Great-Aunt Flora needing her prescription refill at once, which would no doubt inspire them to speedier efforts at locating my quarry.

I had told a similarly fanciful tale to a sympathetic young clerk at the local moving company. She in turn had promised to search through the last month's paperwork for evidence of the vanishing old ladies.

Meanwhile, on a hunch, I'd obtained a list of all the hotels in the Cayman Islands, and was systematically calling them to see if Flora Dabney and her cohorts were in hiding there. I think it was extremely ungrateful of Bill to be churlish about my use of his phone line. Even when I told him I'd pay his miserable little long-distance bill, he wasn't the least bit gracious about it.

Now, though, he looked as if he was regretting having put a stop to my phone inquiries. He was nodding into the phone with a decidedly agitated expression, and saying, "Yes, Mr. Trowbridge," about six times a minute.

"Well, actually, I'm still looking into that last question of yours, Mr. Trowbridge," Bill said, with the hollow laugh he uses when he's lying. "I wanted to make sure I covered all the ramifications for you. But you can certainly give me another question now. Certainly. That's what I'm here for. What would you like to know this week?" He began to scribble notes on his yellow legal pad, grimacing as he wrote.

After a few more minutes of sickening politeness, he hung up the phone and threw his pencil up in the air, making absolutely no attempt to catch it.

I retrieved the pencil for him, setting it carefully on his desk, and waiting to see if he would throw it again, at which point I planned to suggest that he purchase a dog.

"That was Mr. Trowbridge," said Bill. "His wife put us on retainer to answer stupid legal questions for him. He has a very fertile mind—by which I mean that it is absolutely full of crap. He never seems to run out."

"What is it this time?" I asked, to humor him. At least he was talking.

"He wants me to find out—get this: can an Indian tribe confiscate your property if they prove that their tribe once owned the land? If there's an Indian burial or something on your property. He says that Israel seems to have used that logic to establish their nation, and he wants to know if it would work for the Shawnees."

"How would he go about finding a Shawnee?" I asked. I knew that Cherokees were still around, but I thought that most of the other eastern Indian tribes had vanished.

"It may be hypothetical," said Bill. "Or Mr. Trowbridge may be planning to declare himself the last of the tribe, and claim—who knows what? Monticello? Downtown Richmond?"

"I see. Good luck figuring out that answer," I said. "Well, not the answer. It's pretty clear that the answer is no. Nonpayment of taxes for a few centuries would disqualify them, if nothing else, but I suppose he wants the terms of some obscure treaty. It's the whys and wherefores that will take time."

"I haven't *got* time," said Bill. "I need to work on this house sale business before the bar association—"

The phone rang again, and Bill snatched it up with a hunted look on his face. "MacPherson and Hill!" he bleated. Then his face fell and he heaved a mighty sigh. "Oh, hello, Mother."

I was poised to take the phone, thinking surely she must want to speak to me, her only daughter just back from Europe; but Bill ignored my presence, looking more miserable with every breath.

"Yes, Mother. I guess I was supposed to be in court today to see about that restraining order we filed against Dad about the goldfish, but something came up. What? Well, another case, actually. No, Mother, I don't think your case is trivial at all. I *do* like goldfish, it's just that— Well, I don't care what your friend Frances told you, I . . . What? Fine! I hope you can afford him!"

"What was that all about?" I asked when the sound of a receiver being slammed down stopped ringing in my ears.

"I thought you were supposed to be unobtrusive!" Bill said with a snarl. "What are you? A backseat lawyer? If you must know, that was one of my clients. A Mrs. Margaret MacPherson, who shares many of your less attractive traits, such as a tendency to nag. And since you ask, she fired me from her divorce proceedings against my father. Our father. Are you happy now?"

"You haven't told them about the mess you're in, have you?"

Bill put his head in his hands. "No. I have not told my mommy and daddy that I am in imminent danger of going to jail for legal malpractice. I thought they might have enough to worry about as it is. A goldfish custody hearing, perhaps."

I began to pace, which in Bill's cubbyhole does not burn up too many calories. "I can't believe Mother actually fired you, Bill. She always liked you best."

"Yeah, right," sneered my brother. "In her current mood, she considers Jack the Ripper just an average guy. She'll probably hire a woman lawyer now. I wonder if Powell would take the case. At least she's competent."

"You're all right," I said. "You're honest, anyhow. That's a start."

"It is if I can prove it. Right now I'm popularly supposed to have a million bucks salted away in the Cayman Islands." He was out of his seat and through the door before I could protest.

"Where are you going?" I called after him.

"To the courthouse law library!" said Bill. "To check on Shawnee property laws."

◆   ◆   ◆

DOUG MACPHERSON SAGGED against a park bench, listening to his heartbeat. He thought that if he took off his sweat-soaked T-shirt, he could *watch* his heart beat. A masochistic generation, these youngsters of the nineties. In his day, once you finished with boot camp, you tried not to exert yourself unduly and you certainly didn't consider it recreation. But Caroline had insisted. Well, she hadn't *nagged*; she had simply assumed that he would be as addicted to running as she was. And of course, physical exercise was so *good* for him. At the moment, though, all it seemed good for was ensuring that he would look fit and trim in his coffin!

Out of the corner of his eye, he could see Caroline prancing back to see what was keeping him, little beads of sweat glistening on her golden forehead. He tried to subdue his breathing into a controlled wheeze so that she wouldn't see his shoulders shaking with the effort.

"Hi, hon!" she said, handing him the towel from around her neck. "You didn't get a leg cramp, did you?"

"Yes!" he gasped, thankfully seizing the excuse. It sounded better than the total collapse he was experiencing. He eased himself down on the park bench and began massaging his calf. *The right one,* he thought. *I must remember which one to limp on.* Aloud he said, "That darned calf muscle. It's an old football injury from my days on the varsity at Georgia Tech." (Well, he had attended Georgia Tech, and he had played varsity in high school, so it was almost true.)

Caroline pushed her dark bangs away from her forehead. Her lovely, vacant face furrowed with concern. "Gee, can you walk on it, Doug?"

"I can manage," he said, still a trifle breathless. "I probably ought to take it easy for a while, though. Wouldn't want to tear the muscle."

He allowed Caroline to put her shoulder under his arm and guide him along, as he hopped and limped back to the car. "Well, I guess that puts the kibosh on running for a while," he remarked, trying to mute the cheerfulness in his tone. "Maybe I could teach you to play bridge this week instead."

Caroline wrinkled her nose. "Yecch! I hate card games. They're so dreary."

Doug felt a pang of disappointment. He quite enjoyed a rousing game of bridge, and what's more he was good at it. He and Margaret almost always won a prize at the—he choked off the memory in mid-thought. That was the old Doug MacPherson, he reminded himself. If he was going to start over, he couldn't live in the past. Besides, with Caroline there were better things to do than play cards. He pictured poor Margaret at home, watching soap operas and counting the gold-fish, and sighed to himself, thinking how close he had come to death from sheer boredom.

"The leg feels better now," he told Caroline. "Let's try it again."

◆   ◆   ◆

I WAS SITTING AROUND watching the phone not ring and wonder-ing if one could have an early hamburger in lieu of Scotland's very civilized afternoon teatime when the door to the outer office banged, and a beautiful blonde walked in. *Oh, goody,* I thought. *Can fistfights and shots of rye be far behind?* Alas, women's lives never live up to men's fantasies.

She was very pretty in a wholesome track-team sort of way, with short-cropped hair and blue eyes that didn't have time to be charming because they were boring into you for analysis. I endeavored to look pleasant, but since she was probably the sort of person accustomed to being fawned over, my effort made little impression. "May I help you?"

She frowned in my direction and then looked wildly around the of-fice. "Good grief! Edith hasn't resigned, has she?"

"Not to my knowledge," I assured her. "But she isn't here. I'm Eliza-beth MacPherson. Can I help?"

She stopped pacing for a moment and stuck out her hand. "A. P. Hill. I'm your brother's partner. I guess you know that."

I nodded. What I didn't know was whether Bill had confided his current legal difficulties to her. "He's in the courthouse, I think. Mr. Trowbridge called with another legal question."

A. P. Hill rolled her eyes. "I knew Bill should never have taken that stupid job. He'll end up spending all his time ferreting out answers to useless questions—and he'll neglect the real practice. I can't stick around to keep him working on more productive matters because I have an out-of-town trial to deal with." She sighed. "How is he?"

"Oh, he's keeping busy," I said somewhat evasively. "How is your case going? I heard it was a murder trial."

"It's a tough one," she said. "Of course, it's my first real trial, which makes it even more difficult for me."

"They trusted you with a murder trial?" I didn't mean to sound unflattering, but I wouldn't want to risk my life in the hands of a novice attorney.

"Nobody else wanted to take it." She shrugged. "By the time I'm through, it'll hardly pay minimum wage. But I thought that if I did well for Tug Mosier, I could get myself noticed in local legal circles."

"How's the plan going so far?"

"I haven't evolved any brilliant schemes for the defense. He was drunk at the time he supposedly killed his girlfriend, so I had a doctor give him a regression-therapy drug to see if it would help him recall the events of that night."

"What if he remembered doing it?"

A. P. Hill fiddled with a pencil from the desk. "I would have pleaded diminished capacity, I guess. It certainly wouldn't be first-degree murder. I was hoping he'd remember *not* doing it. It could have been a burglar, you know. I needed some kind of evidence that somebody else could have done it."

"Reasonable doubt?"

"Yes. And I got it. Under sedation, Tug remembered a guy named Red going home with him. After that, he just stared at the wall and wouldn't talk. I thought about trying again, but then I remembered one of my law professors saying that you don't really want to know if your client is guilty, because it will detract from the zeal of your defense of him."

"But I thought the whole point of the sedation was to find out if he did it."

"Well, it was, but when I heard him mention another man at the scene of the crime, I thought the safest thing was to go with that. All I have to do is suggest to a jury that Red could have done it, and then they can't convict Tug."

"They can't?"

A.P. groaned. "Of course they can. The jury can do whatever it wants. It's my job to persuade them that they aren't sure enough to convict Tug."

"It would be interesting to know if he did it or not," I mused. "Do you have the paperwork on the case?"

"Copies in the file cabinet. Why?"

"I thought I'd take a look at the autopsy report. I'm a forensic anthropologist."

A. P. Hill did not look particularly impressed by this announcement. "I'll get it for you," she said. "Just leave it on my desk when you're through. I have to go." She scribbled a telephone number on a note pad and wrote *Powell* beside it. "That's the phone number of the motel I'm staying in. I moved out of the old one because they kept forgetting to give me my messages."

"I'll see that Bill gets this," I promised.

"Thanks. While you're at it, tell Bill to start boning up on discrimination law in his copious free time. When this trial is over, I'll have a new case for us."

"A new client?"

She grinned. "Yeah. Me. We're suing the National Park Service."

Before I could ask her what she meant by that, she was gone. I started to leaf through the stack of papers. The case seemed rather ordinary, I thought. Very tragic for the family of the victim, but not exceptional for an attorney or a policeman. It was the sort of case you read about in small-town papers every Monday morning: drunken good old boy kills his girlfriend. I thought prison might not be such a bad idea for Tug Mosier. He didn't seem to have any other prospects.

I hadn't got very far in the case file when the phone rang again.

"Bill MacPherson, please," said a voice like old razor blades.

"I'm sorry, he's not here. May I take a message?" I didn't want to talk to this voice long enough to explain who I wasn't. He sounded like the kind of man who thinks *female* and *secretary* are synonymous anyhow.

"This is Agent Runge of the State Bureau of Investigation. When do you expect Mr. MacPherson to return?"

"Any time now," I said as pleasantly as I could while my blood froze. "Shall I have him call you?"

"You do that." He barked out his number and then hung up without saying goodbye. He probably thought I was scum just because I answered the phone for one of his suspects. I actually felt guilty when I hung up. In fact, I think if the agent had walked in at that point, I might have confessed to two robberies and an earthquake. I'll bet Mr. Runge is pretty darned good at his job.

I made a note to Bill to call SBI Agent Runge at the number given. *Do not whimper into phone,* I added. I thought Bill ought to be warned.

Things were getting serious, though. It looked as though we were running out of time. I called some more moving companies and finally found one who remembered the old ladies. Yes, they had gone out to the Phillips Mansion and packed up all the furniture. Where had they taken it? I asked breathlessly, ready to solve the case.

"It's in storage," the man said. "We are waiting for further instructions."

Old ladies: three. MacPhersons: nothing.

Spurred on by the ominous SBI agent and the cleverness of our opponents, I thought furiously for a while. Where would they go? How would they get there? Did they have a car? Maybe they bought one. How many car dealerships are there in Danville? Wait. If they didn't have a car, how did they get to a dealership? Are there taxis in Danville? I grabbed for the phone book. It was going to be a long afternoon. I could tell that this was going to be tedious. If I had wanted to go around asking prying questions of total strangers, I would have become a social worker.

◆　◆　◆

WITH ALL EIGHTEEN POUNDS of silver-striped Beauregard purring contentedly on her lap, Anna Douglas squinted at her sketch pad and looked again at the swirl of colors in the seascape in front of her. She really did have a lovely view from the patio of her room at the Comfort Inn. The motel was set parallel between the island's main road and the ocean, so that every room offered a sea view. Anna, Jenny, and Julia Hotchkiss had adjoining ground-floor rooms with kitchenettes and sliding glass doors leading to small concrete patios. They were lounging in the salt air, with Anna sketching, Jenny dozing, and Julia working her way through a box of saltwater taffy.

Anna thought the island was most satisfactory. The few little shops on the island were all within walking distance of the motel, and the nearest restaurant had proved satisfactory. The latest issue of *Home Guide* that she'd found in the restaurant advertised several suitable

one-story houses for sale on the island, but decisions regarding perma-
nent residence would have to wait until the others arrived with the car.
True, the island was a bit too crowded with summer tourists, and the
one main road was clogged with cars, but there were compensations for
these inconveniences. Winter would be very pleasant in this summer
climate, a far cry from the bitter chill of Virginia. When the chauffeured
car had brought the three of them on the long drive from the airport,
Anna had decided to take up temporary residence in the Comfort Inn
while she waited for Flora and the others to arrive. They had determined to meet at the island's post office (across the street) at noon two
days hence.

Meanwhile, Anna had busied herself by locating a licensed practical
nurse to look after the two invalids and finding out the particulars of
community life: distance to hospital, location of local churches, and so
on. She took long walks around the island, noting landmarks and FOR
SALE signs. Most of the island's population seemed to be elderly, which
pleased her immensely.

It was by no means certain that the group would decide to stay there
once they were reunited, but Anna hoped that she could persuade them
to do so. Anna never liked to feel that she was without a home. When
she was a young girl, during the Great Depression, her parents had lost
their home, and the memory of that banishment had remained in her
mind all these years, like a shadow on an X ray. She thought she hadn't
minded so much losing the Danville mansion because the others kept
assuring her that there was plenty of money to purchase another house.
But now that she had been a transient for a while, the old feelings of
sleeplessness and nagging anxiety had crept back. She wished that Flora
would hurry up and get there so that they could get settled.

Anna looked down at her sketch pad. In the middle of the placid
ocean, she had drawn the dorsal fin of a shark.

◆   ◆   ◆

THERE'S AN OLD COUNTRY SONG that says, "It's a mighty
rough road from Lynchburg to Danville." It certainly is, especially if
you have to do it by telephone, calling every car dealership in between.
Having just done that, I believe I'd rather try it next time in the runaway freight train.

After many hours of absolutely cloying charm (which does not come naturally to me, despite my Southern upbringing) I managed to find a car dealer in Lynchburg who clearly remembered selling a Chrysler to a gaggle of old ladies who arrived by taxi and paid cash for their purchase. He didn't know where they were headed, though, and I didn't think that I could persuade the police to put out an all-points bulletin for a nonstolen car. Especially since I had no real evidence that the new owners were the old ladies from the Home for Confederate Women. According to the dealer, the car had been purchased by a woman calling herself Mrs. James Ewell Brown. Very funny. I guess they left off the general's last name because that would have been too obvious. If they had added *Stuart*, even a car dealer might have figured out that Mrs. Jeb Stuart was probably an alias. And what were the rest of them calling themselves? Mrs. Lee, Mrs. Jackson, and Mrs. Bedford Forrest? Actually, I was beginning to feel a sneaking admiration for the feisty old dears, and if it hadn't been for the imminent prospect of my brother's going to prison, I might have been tempted to wish them Godspeed and forget the whole thing. As it was, I thought I'd better find them and try to work out a compromise thereafter.

It was nearly seven o'clock. Midnight in Scotland. I decided to call Cameron and give him a report on the situation thus far.

"I thought it would be you," he said. "Even before I heard that four-syllable hello of yours. Nobody else would call at this hour."

"Blame the time zone," I told him. "I've been working all afternoon and couldn't spare a moment earlier."

"How are things in the colonies? I trust your parents are well?"

"I trust so, too," I said. "I haven't had time to contend with them yet. I'm not looking forward to it, either, mind you. But Bill's problems had to come first."

"And have you solved all the troubles of Clan MacPherson? Cleared your brother's name, and all that?"

"Not yet I haven't." I told him all about Bill's ill-fated house sale and the ensuing chaos when both the residents and the purchase money went missing, leaving Bill looking like a swindler with both an irate buyer and the assistant state director of art and antiquities after his hide. "The old ladies are still missing, and so is the money. If only I could find them, I could sort all this out. I managed to track them to

Lynchburg. They took a taxi there and bought a white Chrysler from a local car dealer. Where they went after that is anybody's guess."

"North Carolina, I expect," said Cameron. "And then South Carolina."

"What?"

"You said it was anybody's guess," he replied smugly.

"Don't confuse me," I warned him. "There isn't much time left. Already SBI agents are calling here asking for Bill in ominous tones."

"Well, then you'd better get busy, dear."

"Doing what?"

"Begin by returning a call from your cousin Geoffrey. He rang up earlier this evening for you. I told him you were in America."

"Geoffrey! I certainly don't have time to bother with him right now."

"Nevertheless, you ought to call him. Because he told me that he met a group of old ladies who knew Bill, and that in his opinion they were behaving oddly."

"Where is he?" I whispered. Geoffrey has the most maddening habit of being in the right place at the right time.

"Geoffrey? He's in Atlanta. Shall I give you the number he left?"

"Yes, please," I said evenly. "I'm going to hang up now and call him. And I only wish it were midnight in Atlanta." Not that the lateness of the hour would inconvenience my cousin. Midnight is the shank of his evening. I dialed his number with shaking fingers, because there was an excellent chance that he was out at dinner or partying. (Geoffrey's last quiet evening at home was believed to have taken place in 1983 during a flu epidemic.) Sure enough, the phone rang about ten times and nobody picked it up. I figured I had about five hours to kill before Geoffrey tottered in from his revelries, so I hung up, and cast about for something else to keep me occupied.

I went over and inspected the bookcase. Bill didn't keep any books or magazines worth reading in his office, and Edith's crossword puzzle books didn't interest me either. I was about to go up to Bill's apartment to watch television, not a pleasant prospect, because he has a tiny black-and-white set with no vertical hold. Surely there must be something else I could do, I thought. Short of dusting the office.

Suddenly I noticed the manila folder that A. P. Hill had left with me: the autopsy report on her murder case. I settled back in Bill's chair and began to sift through the report. It began, as they often do, with "the body of a well-nourished female." I suppose that's a holdover from earlier decades when well-nourished bodies were less commonplace. I wondered, though, if some of my yogurt-happy jogger friends would merit some other opening remark. *This is the body of a downright scrawny yuppie . . .* It was a pleasant fantasy, enlivening an otherwise unpleasant chronicle of a young life wasted.

Misti Hale had been twenty-four years old at the time of her death. The report went on to describe the lividity of the body, the coloration, the bruises on her neck. I read through the report and looked at the photographs of the girl who might have been pretty. In graduate school I'd had courses in forensic pathology, and all this looked sadly familiar. I kept thinking, though, that there was something else I should be looking for, but I couldn't remember what it was. All my notes were back in Scotland anyhow. I was about to put the folder aside, thinking that the missing detail might come back to me later, when the phone rang. I hoped it was Bill. I hadn't had dinner.

"Calvin Trowbridge here," said a male voice laden with Southern money. "Is Bill there?"

"It's nearly eight o'clock," I said, glancing at my watch. "He's not in the office. Is it urgent?"

"No, just a thought. See, I have Bill on retainer to—"

"Oh, you're the one! Well, he's terribly busy. Why don't *you* go to law school if you're so keen to know all this stuff?"

I hung up before he could reply. I had considered many careers during my four-year stint as a liberal arts major, but public relations was never one of them.

◆ ◆ ◆

AT TEN O'CLOCK I gave up on Bill and went back to my motel room. (I could have stayed with my brother, but lodging two people in his apartment would be like trying to live in a squirrel's nest.) I was still thinking about A. P. Hill's case and trying to come up with more ideas for tracing the old ladies. Washing my hair did not get me any further along on either problem.

I waited until nearly midnight before trying to return Geoffrey's call. The chances of waking him up were slim, but I'd hope for the best.

After two rings he picked up the phone, sounding as disgustingly bright and cheerful as ever.

"This is your cousin from Scotland," I told him. "And don't make any snide remarks about Queen Elizabeth I calling Mary Queen of Scots that, because I'm in no mood for Trivial Pursuit."

"Actually, it was James I to whom she referred," purred Geoffrey, "but I wouldn't dream of wasting your time with intellectual banter. You haven't the gift for it. I did just want to tell you a story that might interest you. Cameron hinted that there were family problems in the Old Dominion. Would you care to elaborate?"

"No. If you have anything useful to tell me, I'll feed your hunger for gossip. Otherwise you will have to depend on supermarket tabloids for your weekly quota of sleaze. Now what's so important that you called Scotland to talk to me about it?"

"Actually my main reason for phoning was to see if you knew anything about the Lime Kiln Theatre in Lexington. They have a wonderful repertory company and put on a series of plays—"

"Yes, I know about them, Geoffrey. I suppose you were thinking of auditioning?"

"Well, I thought I might enjoy the acting experience. And I'd much rather spend a summer in Virginia than in Manhattan. Besides, they do a play called *Stonewall Country* about the Civil War, and I thought I might try out for the role of Jeb Stuart."

"Rubbish! He was a general. You're too young to play a general."

"*Au contraire*, my little Visigoth. Jeb Stuart became a general at the age of twenty-nine. And he was by all accounts colorful and handsome. I am perfectly suited to the role."

"He was a braggart and a show-off," I conceded. "So there might be some justification in casting you in the part. I'd like to see you engulfed in a red beard. But I'm sure you didn't call me to discuss your acting career."

"No. That was only to give you some background so you'd understand why I was at Stone Mountain wearing a Confederate uniform."

I sighed. "No, Geoffrey. Even with the background you provided, I cannot make that leap. Why the devil *were* you trick-or-treating in a state park?"

"Have you ever been to Stone Mountain? On the side of it is a huge bas-relief of Lee and his generals. Quite inspiring. I'd driven down to

Atlanta to visit all the historical sites and also to visit a wonderful costume shop in the Underground, where I found quite a fetching Confederate uniform, in which I look unutterably dashing."

"Let me guess. You bought this Confederate uniform. Did it have a fringed gold sash and a plumed hat, by any chance? I thought so. And you just could not resist nipping down to Stone Mountain to prance around—"

"Do you want to hear this or not?"

"Oh, all right. Go ahead."

"That's better. Where was I? Oh, yes. Stone Mountain. I was strolling in the parking lot, trying to get the feel of being a general, when a little old lady came up to me and admired my uniform. We started to chat, and when I told her about my hopes of going to do theatre in Lexington, she said that she and her friends were from Virginia, and of course I asked what town, and she said Danville, and then we played Southern chess: do you know my friend-so-and-so?"

"Old ladies?" I was suddenly interested. "Were there eight of them?"

"I only counted five," said Geoffrey. "But the one I talked to knew Bill. After a moment she seemed to realize that admitting this had been a mistake. She became decidedly uneasy. And then her friend came along and hustled her off before I could find out what was going on. It seemed fairly strange to me, because usually little old ladies want to talk your ear off, and they'll tell you their life stories without the least provocation, so I wondered why this lot was so evasive."

"Well, the State Bureau of Investigation would like a word with them, for starters," I said. "They seem to think that Bill murdered them." I explained the simple little house sale to Geoffrey.

"And people wonder why chivalry is dead," he murmured. "So they conned Virginia out of a million five and left Bill to talk to the authorities. That would explain why they seemed so fidgety."

"Where were they going?"

"By the time I asked that, the old lady's bossy friend had turned up and was trying to elbow her toward their car. She said they were going to an island to meet friends."

"Probably the other three fugitives," I said.

"Well, I did ask who they were going to see, because they were acting as suspicious as all get-out, but I had to make my question charming and innocent-sounding, on account of their nervous states. As she walked away, the sweet old lady said, 'We'll be visiting Major Edward Anderson.' I remember the name because he was a comedian that Captain Grandfather used to like, but it seemed odd to me that they'd be visiting an old-time comedian."

"Maybe they knew him. Would he be about their age?"

"I'm sure he was much older. He played Rochester on the old Jack Benny show. And I never heard anybody call him major. I knew that the old dears were trying to be vague, but sometimes people tell bits of the truth when they're trying to be misleading."

"And some people are misleading when they're trying to tell the truth."

"Well, I thought it was worth looking into. If I could do it without expending any particular effort."

"You've never been mistaken for Mother Teresa, have you?" I asked, but sarcasm is wasted on Geoffrey.

"Don't be ungrateful. I called Mother to see if she knew an Edward Anderson, thinking he might be a politician or a social lion in Georgia, but she'd never heard of him. I suppose I could consult a library, if it's a question of Cousin Bill going to prison." Geoffrey yawned, not from the lateness of the hour, but at the prospect of exerting himself on someone else's behalf.

"I'll see what I can find out," I told him. "But feel free to pursue the matter if the spirit moves you, Geoffrey."

"There's not a reward out for the old dears, is there?"

"No. Everyone else thinks Bill has murdered them. I suppose we could call you to testify if it comes to that."

"I saw only five of them," he pointed out. "He could have murdered the other three."

"Thank you for that vote of family confidence, Geoffrey. I'll take it from here."

"Good. And if I'm cast as Jeb Stuart, you will come and see the show, won't you?"

"I wouldn't miss it." *I'll be rooting for the Yankees.*

◆　◆　◆

After that I went to sleep, but I must still have been reviewing the events of the day because I kept dreaming about making phone calls and trying to find Misti Hale's name in the phone book so I could call her up and ask her how she died. Something must have been percolating through my subconscious, though, because around six A.M. I sat bolt upright in bed, realizing that I had been mulling over that autopsy report and that there was something odd about it. It might have been a simple omission of a detail on the part of the coroner, but it wasn't there. If A. P. Hill was any good at all at being a lawyer, she could take that fact and run with it. I wondered if I could catch her before she left the motel.

I drove back to Bill's, marveling at how little traffic there was. Of course it was six forty-five in the morning, and I don't suppose that rush hour in Danville starts until about five to eight. I had my pick of parking places.

I pounded on the door to Bill's tiny apartment, knowing that he had to have heard me. No place in his apartment is all that far from the door. "Open up, Bill!" I called out. "It's your sister. Without a search warrant."

The door opened a fraction, and I could see rumpled blond hair and an unshaven face peering out at me. "What do you want?" he asked between yawns.

"The key to your office and a cup of tea," I said sweetly. "I see that I woke you. No rush. Any time in the next minute or so will do."

Bill glared. "Why do you want the key?"

"To call your law partner. I have some information that may help her case."

"*Her* case?" he wailed. "What about me?"

"I'm still working on it." I snatched the key and fled downstairs.

A few minutes later, I was talking to A. P. Hill, who was wide awake at this hour, as I suspected she would be. She probably alphabetizes her underwear drawer. "I looked over that coroner's report, and I have some information for you," I said after the initial civilities.

"I don't see what you could have found without doing any lab work," she said.

"They did the lab work. And either they forgot to record one significant finding or there's something strange about Misti Hale's death."

"You mean she wasn't strangled?"

"Sort of. There were bruises on her neck, all right, and her body had been in the car for a couple of days, so the lividity and coloration weren't much help, but what I would expect to find noted on the report was evidence of petechial hemorrhaging."

"Which is?"

"Red dots, especially noticeable in the eyes. They are actually small hemorrhages in the capillaries under the skin, and the condition is most evident in the whites of the eyes. The pressure put on the blood vessels during strangulation causes the tiny ruptures. But in the autopsy report on Misti Hale, no petechial hemorrhages were mentioned."

"But you said there were bruises on her neck."

"Right, but if there weren't any hemorrhages, then she didn't die from that. In grad school, we heard about a case like this. I have a hunch that Misti Hale was one of those rare and unlucky people whose blood pressure goes down under stress instead of up. You know, like a possum."

"She passed out?"

"*Way* out. Someone took her by the throat, and she went into shock almost immediately. Her blood pressure plummeted and her heart stopped. So she didn't die from strangulation, but from shock. It would have been very fast. Seconds."

A. P. Hill was not impressed with my diagnosis. "Hmm," she said. "But whoever had his hands around her throat still killed her."

"Maybe not on purpose. Her assailant might have stopped in a couple of seconds. He may have been trying to shut her up. But she had this blood pressure trouble, and she passed out and died. It's not conclusive proof, but you could argue that it was not an intentional homicide. You could get expert witnesses to back you for manslaughter."

"He might get off with time served for that." A. P. Hill sounded thoughtful. "And I could get expert witnesses to testify to this condition."

"Sure. If I were you, I'd start calling the UVA med school and go from there."

"Thanks. I'll look into it. Unless you'd like to—"

"Sorry. I have to figure out what Major Edward Anderson is doing on a Georgia island."

"Friend of yours?" The disinterest was back in her voice.

"No. Somebody mentioned it, and I got curious." I was tempted to tell her about Bill's problem, but he would have killed me for betraying his confidence.

"Major Edward Anderson. Well, there's the famous one, of course."

"The comedian. Rochester. I thought of that."

"Comedian? Oh, on Jack Benny. No, that was *Eddie* Anderson. I was talking about the Confederate officer. Wasn't he in charge of battery positions at the beginning of the war?"

"Where?"

"I don't know. He was only a major. But in my office there are some reference books on the Civil War, and bound copies of *Civil War Times Illustrated*. You might check those. Of course it might be the wrong man."

"It's worth a try. Thanks."

Twenty minutes later, I was reshelving all of Powell Hill's reference books when Bill came in, holding two steaming mugs of tea.

"Took you long enough," I said. "Unfortunately, I can't drink it."

"Why not?" His tone suggested that I had just refused the Holy Grail.

"Because there aren't that many rest areas between here and I-95," I told him as I started out the door. "I think I've found your old ladies."

"Order A. P. Hill to prepare for action!"
—NEXT-TO-LAST WORDS OF
THOMAS J. (STONEWALL) JACKSON,
MAY 10, 1863

"Tell Hill he must *come up."*
—NEXT-TO-LAST WORDS OF
ROBERT E. LEE, OCTOBER 1870

GILES COUNTY, VIRGINIA,
DECEMBER 1901

G A B R I E L   H A W K S   T R A C E D his forefinger along a line of type
in the Richmond newspaper. His eyes weren't what they used to be—
and he never had been much on reading—but the name of his old
friend had jumped out at him from the columns of gray words: Tom
Bridgeford . . . state senator . . . appointed to the board of the
newly established Home for Confederate Women in Danville. He tried
to picture the lanky young sailor as a dignified old politician, but the

image wouldn't come. Even though his own mirror showed him an image of an arthritic old man of fifty-five, he couldn't picture Tom any older than twenty-five, still chafing under the weight of authority and spoiling for a fight. If he was a senator now, and active in charitable works, he must have prospered.

Gabriel Hawks looked about the simple parlor of the farmhouse, with its sepia photograph of General Lee over the mantel and a home-made braided rug on the pine floor. He reckoned that he hadn't done too well, as the world measured success, but by his own lights he'd had a good life. He had done a bit of wandering in Georgia in the aftermath of the war, and then he'd made his way back to Giles County and taken up farming again at the homeplace. The community was much the poorer, mostly because it had lost most of the boys he'd grown up with, but he was happy enough back in the sheltering mountains of the Blue Ridge. Shortly after his return he had married Mary Hadden, who, at sixteen, had been left widowed by the War. She had lived to see the beginning of the new century, but pneumonia had taken her during the first weeks of winter, and now Gabriel was alone again. There had been no children to keep him company in his old age, and keep the family land. He supposed he was free now, and about as old as he was likely to get. Surely he would soon be joining Mary in the sweet hereafter. Until then he could have his heart's desire, if he wished it, or at least what there was of it that money could buy. *What are you waiting for, Gabe?* said a voice in his head. It sounded like young Tom's voice, urging him on.

He stared into the fireplace and thought about those far-off days in Georgia when the world had about gone to hell around them. There he was, waving farewell to Tom Bridgeford and cantering off down a dusty road with a fortune in gold in a saddlebag. Bridgeford—*State Senator Bridgeford*—must have made it back with his, and from the sound of his prosperous life, he had put it to good use. Old Tom would probably laugh to learn that his old shipmate was still a poor mountain farmer in the Blue Ridge. "You could have made something of yourself, Hawks," he'd say, if he knew. But Gabriel hadn't wanted to try. He missed the farm and he was more than a little afraid that bushwhackers would get him if he tried to head home with the gold. And how would he explain the gold to the folks back in Giles without sounding like a vulture picking at the bones of the Confederacy? There was hardly a family in the valley that hadn't lost someone to the cause. How could he profit from the sorrow and still look them in the eyes?

But he couldn't give it back, either. He didn't see that the new government would put it to good use. Likely as not, they'd try to hang him for having taken it in the first place. Besides, the day might come when he would need the money—to pay taxes or buy new livestock after a bitter winter, or for the children he thought would come. He'd wandered down to the coast with some notion of trying to work his way out of the country by ship, but that wouldn't have been safe either. Not with a knapsack full of gold. Near Brunswick, he'd made his way to a little island that was mostly marshland and sand dunes, and there he had buried his gold bars. He marked the spot, fixing it in his mind with landmarks. He reasoned that he could always go back to get them if the need ever arose.

That had been thirty-six years ago. Many's the time Hawks had toyed with the idea of going back for the gold. He dreamed of building a fine house for Mary or buying a new herd of dairy cows, but each time he thought of making the long journey south again, he always abandoned the project. His need was not great enough to offset the perils of the journey and the fear of discovery.

Now he was old, and Mary was sleeping under a headstone in the churchyard. It was too late in life for riches now. There was no place he wanted to go and nothing he wanted other than what he had. It seemed a shame, though, for the gold to be left in the sands of Georgia. It put him in mind of the parable about the servant who buried his talents and was scolded by the Master for not making use of them. He looked again at the newspaper article about the prosperous Senator Bridgeford. Tom was always the smart one; he had always known what they should do. Gabriel would write his old comrade and tell him where the gold was. Surely a man so prosperous and wise would know what best to do with it.

He pressed his face close to a sheet of writing paper and began to spell out the words: *Dear Tom Bridgeford—I take pen in hand to write you this missive . . .*

*"Many are the hearts that are weary tonight, wishing
for the war to cease . . ."*
— *"Tenting Tonight,"* CIVIL WAR SONG
SUNG BY BOTH ARMIES

CHAPTER

9

THE FASTEST WAY to Georgia is Interstate 95, which is an extremely boring road—a more or less straight line of asphalt running down the coastal plain, hemmed in by an endless stretch of pine barrens and sandy soil. There is nothing in the way of scenery to keep you alert unless your reading taste runs to garish billboards or lists of fast-food joints at forthcoming exit ramps. I figured that the drive from southeast Virginia to southeast Georgia would be six hours of unbroken monotony, but much as I dreaded it, I will admit that there are routes I am even more reluctant to travel, roads that are anything but boring. These roads are mostly north of Danville.

I have an old school friend who lives in western Maryland, and the drive up I-81 to her house is always an anxious journey for me. To get to Frederick, I must pass through the heartland of the War. First comes Lexington, where Stonewall Jackson taught artillery at Virginia Military Institute before he went forth in 1861 to practice it. An hour or so north is New Market, where the young boys of VMI still in their school uniforms went up against the Union Army and were butchered. Just seeing the road sign NEW MARKET makes me uneasy, and I picture schoolboys dying in the long grass of the valley. Farther up are exits for Charles Town, West Virginia, which means horse racing to most people nowadays, but to me, it conjures up an image of John Brown, waiting for the rope to be placed around his neck and predicting the coming war with his dying words. I-81 is a modern four-lane highway, but it follows the old route along the valley, where the armies traveled under Sheridan and Jackson, and I feel their presence, even over the roar of the eighteen-wheelers whizzing past me.

Near the Maryland border I cross Antietam Creek, and the chills start. *Antietam* . . . I know that there are streets in Maryland named that now, probably grade schools and dry cleaners even. But to me Antietam is bodies piled in a roadway, one on top of the other, making a mound twelve feet high, stretching on and on through the dust of that winding road. It is the stench of powder and blood and death that can't still linger after a hundred years and more, but still I smell it.

They are just words on road signs, that's all, I tell myself. And between Norfolk and Richmond, on I-64, is an exit sign for Cold Harbor. *Cold Harbor* . . . The swampy terrain made it almost impossible to attack the well-entrenched Confederate Army. To charge in such a marsh against the enemy's guns was suicide, and the Union soldiers knew it. Cold Harbor. On the shirts of their uniforms, they pinned pieces of paper bearing their names and their hometowns. That way when their bodies were pulled out of the swamp, they could be sent home for burial. One soldier wrote: *June 3, 1864. I was killed.*

I go out of my way not to drive past Cold Harbor.

In the South we haven't really forgotten the War. Many of us knew people who knew people who fought in it. It hasn't quite passed into history yet. It's still more feelings than facts, and likely to remain so for a good while. I know this because I've been with my Scottish husband to an older battlefield—Culloden Moor, west of Inverness—and watched his face grow pale and solemn as he looked at the field where *his* kinsman died. On that field, the Scots met death, defeat, and the end of their country as an independent nation. That was 1746, and it still stirs them, so I figure we have a ways to go before the emotion fades away, before words like *Antietam* and *Cold Harbor* pass without raising chills and dark memories.

I hadn't thought about the War in a long time. It was Bill and his damned Confederate ladies who brought it all back. Even on I-95, where the most ominous sign is an ad for Gatorland, the gray ghosts rode along, making me remember them. In Virginia, the Civil War isn't something you learn in school; it's a Presence. Always there. I can remember an ancient great-aunt telling Bill and me about our great-great-grandfather David MacPherson, a sixteen-year-old private in the 68th Infantry under General Bragg. In 1865 the 68th had marched from Virginia to Fort Fisher in the snow, he'd told her. They had no shoes by that time, just shreds of leather or rags wrapped around cracked and callused feet. It was winter and they followed the railroad tracks south. They left bloody footprints in the snow.

That's the war to me: a starving sixteen-year-old leaving footprints in the snow in his own blood. And the women I was tracking were the daughters of those young soldiers—the last link with them. So what was I supposed to do? Coax those old ladies into a nursing home so the state could take their house?

I wished there was something to look at on I-95 besides a million damned pine trees. I didn't want to have to think anymore.

◆　◆　◆

A MONTH IN A COUNTY JAIL had not improved Tug Mosier in any way. The lack of sunlight and starchy jail food had made him even paler and more flabby. His hair shone with grease, and a stubble of beard completed a look that would have made a jury convict him on general principles. He looked guilty of *something*. A. P. Hill managed to smile at her scruffy client, hoping that she looked more confident than she felt. At least she had a shred of a defense now.

"How's it going?" she asked.

"I hate being cooped up," said Tug. "Specially in summertime. And I sure as hell could use a drink."

"I can't help you there, but I do have some news about your case. First of all, I just had a meeting with the district attorney. He has offered you a deal, which is really beside the point because I have a new lead that may win this case for us."

"The D.A. is talking a deal?" The scowl left Tug's face and he leaned forward with the first sign of genuine interest he had shown since she arrived.

"Yes. He wants you to plead guilty to second-degree murder. He says he'll ask for a ten-year sentence."

"Yeah, but you don't serve all the time they give you."

"Well, you could, of course, if you tried to escape or didn't behave. But usually a prison term is about a quarter of the sentence. Say two and a half years. That's a long time to be behind bars, I'm sure. But listen: I have great news. I had a forensic expert study the autopsy report on Misti and she came up with a wonderful piece of evidence to help our case."

Powell's voice bubbled with enthusiasm as she explained Elizabeth's theory about the absence of petechial hemorrhaging in Misti Hale. She had to repeat the part about low blood pressure—and still Tug looked unimpressed. "You see," she said triumphantly, "if she died of shock, you didn't kill her intentionally!"

Tug Mosier frowned and rubbed his stubble of beard. "You think a Patrick County jury is going to follow that?" he asked.

"I'll call in a medical expert," A.P. assured him. "We'll go over the whole process. Maybe even have a chart to help the jurors focus on the technical part."

"But if we do that, the district attorney won't be going for second degree, will he? He'll try to convict me of first-degree homicide. Maybe capital murder. They fry people in this state, you know."

"We'd argue that Misti's death was accidental."

"That's just it," said Tug sadly. "We'd argue. But you can lose an argument. You can't lose a negotiated deal. I don't want to bet my life that this jury will understand a word you're saying. *I* didn't, much."

A.P. looked down at her briefcase full of notes, the result of hours of work researching the case. Then she looked at Tug Mosier, stone-faced and flabby, with the stirrings of fear in his eyes. "You want to plead guilty, then?" she asked. "Accept the D.A.'s offer?"

"I reckon so," said Tug. "It seems the best way. I can do two and a half years, no sweat. I got friends inside. And—no offense, ma'am—but this is pretty damn near your first case. I'm not anxious to risk my life on the skills of a baby lawyer. Really: no offense."

"None taken," murmured A. P. Hill. "I'll go back and tell Mr. Hazelit that we'll accept his offer."

Her client settled back in his straight wooden chair with a happy smile. "I sure am glad you're taking this so well, ma'am. I do hate a woman that argues and nags at a fellow. Misti was always a one for that. She used to bitch and moan till I'd itch to slam her through a wall. Anything to shut up that mouth of hers."

A. P. Hill studied Tug Mosier's close-set blue eyes and his expressionless face as he reminisced about his dead lover without a trace of sorrow or regret. "You did it, didn't you?" she whispered.

"Yeah. Reckon I can own up now."

"But why did you agree to the regression technique?"

"Well, I don't really believe in hypnosis and all," said Tug. "Figured if you're strong enough, you can fight it. I thought I'd say I didn't do it and then the doc would testify that I was innocent. Didn't work like that. It scared hell out of me when I came to and you said I'd been talking about Red Dowdy."

"Why? He was there, wasn't he?"

"Yeah. He saw the whole thing. The next day he told me what I did—but I didn't believe him. I had sorta forgot about her being in the trunk."

"But maybe he's lying!" said A.P. eagerly. "Red would hardly admit to you that *he* had committed murder."

"Why not? He's always been straight with me before, about owning up to things. When we robbed that hiker at Hanging Rock, he—" Tug saw her eyes widen. He smiled a little and looked away. "Don't reckon you want to hear about that, ma'am."

She shivered, pondering how the case might have gone in court. She saw herself grandstanding in her best baby-lawyer tradition. Then she envisioned the slow-talking old D.A. getting up in his shiny blue suit and blowing her away without so much as raising his voice. "So there was a witness who could have testified that you were guilty. Do *you* remember what happened?"

He frowned with the effort of concentration. "I sort of remember her yelling and me trying to make her quit. But it was no more than second degree, honest. I just felt like shutting her up, and I was too drunk to care about the consequences. So if I can cut a deal for second degree, I'll take it."

"I'll go tell the district attorney," whispered A. P. Hill, fighting an impulse to run from the room.

"Yeah, tell him it's a deal," said Tug Mosier. "I can do two and a half, Miz Hill. Misti was worth that."

◆   ◆   ◆

JEKYLL ISLAND IS NOW ATTACHED to the mainland of Georgia by an umbilical cord of highway, a manmade isthmus constructed of dirt dredged from the adjoining sound. I didn't think the old ladies would be too hard to find. The island is only a couple of miles long and less than a mile wide. A tollbooth at the end of the ribbon of road charges a small fee for every car coming onto Jekyll.

I got there about ten in the morning after spending a restless night in Savannah. I called Bill to make sure he hadn't been taken into custody —or jumped off a bridge. He sounded despondent (which showed a good grasp of reality, I thought), but at least things weren't any worse than when I left. I told Bill to give me a couple of days to straighten things out. I also asked him to invite our parents to dinner at his apartment on Saturday night. I didn't know whether we would be able to straighten *them* out, but I intended to try. I needed Bill for moral support—and to pitch in with whatever persuasive skills he had managed to glean from law school.

The matter at hand depended on luck—after all, the old ladies might not be on this island at all—but beyond that I didn't foresee too many difficulties. Southern charm and grad student persistence ought to get me through this on my own. At the tollbooth I asked the attendant if he remembered a car full of elderly ladies coming on to the island. He said that he'd be hard-pressed to remember anything *else.* Apparently the temperate south Georgia islands are a great favorite of the over-sixty set.

Trying not to envision a house-to-house inquiry, I drove on, taking the road that encircles the island and getting the general lay of the land. The business district—one row of shops and a post office—was easy enough to find. I decided to complete the circuit of the island and then to center my search on this hundred yards of island. A postmaster could tell me if a new post office box had been rented; the realtor would know if a gaggle of old ladies had been house hunting; and sooner or later they would have to turn up at the little grocery store or the restaurant across the road. I had one advantage, that of surprise. They didn't know that anyone had come looking for them, although I was certain that they were shrewd enough to be cautious anyway. *I* would be, if I were absconding with more than a million dollars.

On the side of the island facing the mainland, I found a historical marker that confirmed my guess about this being the old ladies' destination. I parked the car off the side of the road under a tree and went up to read the marker. According to the sign, Jekyll Island had been the site of Confederate battery positions in 1861, equipped with a 42-pound gun and 32-pound navy guns. The artillery, anchored into earthworks of palmetto logs, timber, sandbags, and railroad cross ties, had been placed there for the protection of Brunswick; but on February 10, 1862, the fortifications had been dismantled, and the guns were sent to Savannah—by a Major Edward Anderson. Apparently the runaway ladies had been reading up on their chosen hideaway.

I was climbing back into the car to head for the tiny business district when a car full of elderly women weaved past me. The silver-haired driver seemed inclined to take her half of the road out of the middle, so I resolved to let them get a good head start before I ventured out on the road. As I watched them go by, though, I realized that the white Chrysler had a Virginia license plate. *Mrs. Jeb Stuart rides again*, I thought, and gunned my car to pursue the fugitives. They were headed north, to the undeveloped marshland part of the island, a haunt of bird-watchers and seascape artists. It wasn't going to be much of a chase, because you can circle Jekyll in twenty minutes if traffic permits.

They pulled off into the sand and piled out of the car. I parked across the road, then strolled over, trying not to look threatening. There were five of them—all well past seventy, I judged—and they were wearing the sort of crepe old-lady dresses that one usually sees at tea parties, not on beach excursions. They paid no attention to me because they were arguing among themselves and trying to haul something out of the trunk of the Chrysler.

"Can I help you ladies?" I said, grateful for an excuse to strike up a conversation.

One of them glared at me suspiciously, but a sweet-faced Helen Hayes type smiled prettily and said that they'd be ever so grateful if I could hoist that old piece of machinery out of the cavernous trunk of their automobile. I peered in to see what was giving them problems, trying not to think about that scene in *The Great Escape* when the Germans pull machine guns out of the truck and mow down the prisoners. These absconding felons looked harmless enough.

"What is this?" I asked between gasps as I hauled a vacuum-cleaner-sized machine out of the trunk.

They looked at each other with worried frowns.

"It's a vacuum cleaner," said the tall, suspicious one.

"We have sand in the backseat of our car," said a short one in a black dress.

Like hell it was a vacuum cleaner. It was a metal detector. In college I'd had a boyfriend who used one to look for Civil War bullets at battlefields. I decided, though, that it would be detrimental to this budding relationship to call the old swindlers *liars* at this stage. It was obvious, though, that they were anxiously awaiting my departure, and I realized that between airline schedules and Virginia grand juries, I really didn't have time to worm my way into their confidence through days of charm and patience. I decided to come straight to the point, a maneuver practically unheard of in Southern circles, but occasionally necessary.

"Which one of you is Flora Dabney?" I asked.

They all gasped, and the sweet-looking one turned to the suspicious one and said, "Don't tell her anything, Flora!" which pretty much settled the identity question right then and there. After an awkward pause, Flora introduced me to her cohorts: Mary Lee Pendleton, Lydia Bridgeford, Dolly Hawks Smith, and Ellen Morrison.

"Where are the others?"

"Back at the inn," said Dolly Smith. "Two of them are invalids. Are you a police officer?"

"I'm Elizabeth MacPherson," I said. "My brother is that naive young attorney who sold your house for you in Danville."

"Such a nice boy," one of them murmured. "He's well, I trust?"

"He's about to be disbarred. Or worse. The buyer of your house just discovered that the state of Virginia had claimed it. So he wants his money back, and everyone thinks Bill has it."

"I can't imagine how you found us," murmured Mary Lee Pendleton, twisting her string of pearls. "We really worked hard on our getaway plans."

"Until you went and blabbed to that young man in uniform at Stone Mountain," said Lydia Bridgeford. "You always were a fool for a handsome man, Mary Lee!"

I motioned to a picnic table set back under the trees. "Let's talk about this," I said. "I need to know exactly what's going on, and I hope I can persuade you to return to Virginia with me."

Flora Dabney shook her head. "We're not going to become prisoners of the state. They've taken our house, haven't they?"

"Yes. And they're about to charge my brother with murdering you." They listened thoughtfully while I explained that no one but Bill had ever seen them, and that there was no proof they were still alive.

"I didn't want to leave a paper trail," said Dolly Smith. "I understand that's very important in the fugitive business. Perhaps I overdid it a bit."

"Your brother is a very nice young man," Ellen Morrison ventured. "I wouldn't want him to get into trouble on our account."

"So you didn't plan this to incriminate Bill?"

Flora Dabney shook her head. "No. The fact that he was so trusting was helpful, of course, but we couldn't have counted on it. You see, we received a notice that the state wanted to take over the Phillips Mansion as an historic building, and that we were to be sent to a nursing home."

"We had to do something!" said Ellen Morrison with a quaver in her voice.

Lydia Bridgeford patted her hair. "I decided to see if there was something we could do. I spend a lot of time at the courthouse doing my genealogical researches—"

"She's almost back to Noah," muttered Dolly Smith.

"So I asked Bonnie—she's the clerk, such a sweet girl—"

"Although perhaps too trusting for a public official," murmured Flora.

"Just Bill's type," I said.

"Well, I watched Bonnie for a while and I learned how things work at the courthouse. All the paperwork goes to Bonnie's desk. When she gets time, she enters the information in the record book by hand and she types it into the computer records. Well, I got to thinking about this, and I realized that if the piece of paper disappeared from Bonnie's desk *before* she entered the information, no one would ever know! I kept going to the courthouse, doing my historical searches, and when Bonnie left for lunch, I'd check through her paperwork. Sure enough, one day the notice of—what was it?"

"Eminent domain," said Dolly Smith.

"So you took the paper before it could be filed anywhere?" I asked. "That means that Bill did the title search correctly. He didn't find any lien on the property because there wasn't one to be found."

"Oh, yes. We knew that *any* lawyer would balk if he found a lien," Mary Lee Pendleton explained. "But we knew we'd have to work fast, before the state did anything else."

"The newspaper ad was my idea," said Flora Dabney. "And I said we'd have to get cash on the barrel head."

"Yes, dear, but the Cayman Islands was my suggestion," said Mary Lee. "You know I asked that kind gentleman banker—"

"But why did you have Bill run the ad and show the house and sign the deed?"

"We didn't want too many people to see us," said Ellen Morrison. "In case they decided to come after us. We didn't want to be caught."

"And now we are," sighed Dolly Smith.

"Rubbish!" said Flora Dabney. "This young lady can't make us go back. She's not a policeman."

"I don't want my brother to go to jail," I said. "But I don't want to see you all go to a nursing home either—if you don't want to."

"Perhaps we could send back some sort of proof that we're still alive —and that Bill is not to blame," Flora said. "Just don't expect us to go back."

"Couldn't you get people to support your cause?" I asked. "Surely the Sons of Confederate Veterans, or perhaps some state politicians—"

Dolly Smith shrugged. "People are afraid of the Confederacy these days. Too many people linked the battle flag with racism, and no one in government wants his name linked with our cause."

"You're politically incorrect," I said.

"I suppose so," sighed Flora. "People do want history to be simple. It is inconvenient to remember that the Southern soldiers used to infuriate the Union ones by calling them abolitionists. Most Yankees deemed it a great insult. They thought they were fighting to preserve the union, just as we assumed that we were fighting for independence. Now, of course, it is more pleasant for people to think otherwise. People do like there to be heroes in their histories."

"My father, Thomas Bridgeford, was a hero," said Lydia stoutly. "He was a great Southern gentleman. Of course, he lost all his money after the crash of '29. He was quite old then, of course, and I've never blamed him."

"Which brings us to this," said Dolly Smith, tapping the metal detector. "I suppose we can tell you about it now. We might need your help."

"Help for what?" I asked. I hoped they weren't looking for World War II land mines to carry on the rebellion.

Flora Dabney smiled and patted my arm. "We're trying to locate the Confederate treasury, dear."

◆   ◆   ◆

EDITH STOOD in the doorway surveying her employer with a worried frown. "You look like the fellow for whom Dismal Swamp was named."

Bill rubbed his eyes and groaned. "Is it too late to consider a career in real estate?"

"Seems like that's what caused your problem in the first place," Edith replied.

"My sister says that I'm too trusting."

Edith considered this statement. "Well," she said. "I don't think this would have happened if A. P. Hill had been here. Maybe you just need to be a little more conservative from now on."

"If there is a now on. If my sister doesn't find Flora and her cohorts, I could be retaining Powell as my defense attorney."

If Edith had a soothing reply to this outburst of self-pity, it was forestalled by the appearance of A. P. Hill herself, briefcase in hand, looking as grimly determined as usual. She wore her no-nonsense blue suit, and her blond hair was newly cropped into the unglamorous style she favored to offset her prettiness. Bill resisted the urge to crawl under his desk in the face of such ruthless efficiency.

"Hello," she said. "My case is finished. We plea-bargained." She took in the bleak expressions on the faces of her listeners. "What are y'all looking so glum about? I'm the one who lost the chance of a great trial."

Bill and Edith looked at each other, avoiding A. P. Hill's searching gaze.

"What's wrong? Did Mr. Trowbridge finally stump you with a question?"

"Tell her," said Edith. "I just remembered we need some more manila folders. I'll run out and get some. It's almost lunchtime anyhow." It was ten-fifteen. She snatched up her purse and hurried out the door before anyone could reply.

A. P. Hill set down her briefcase and perched on the edge of Bill's desk. "Tell me what?" she said with a puzzled frown.

"I had a few problems while you were gone," said Bill. "First of all, I was handling my mother's divorce. You knew about that? Well, my mother fired me. Claims I wasn't devoting enough time to her case."

"Just as well," said Powell. "It's best not to represent family and you probably wouldn't have charged her, so it isn't a financial loss. I guess it hurt your feelings though."

"It might have," said Bill, "except that I had other matters on my mind. Mr. Trowbridge called this morning. He's canceling the rest of the yearly retainer for stupid questions. He says he's decided to take law courses at night at the local community college. He claims that my sister suggested it."

"*That* is a financial loss," murmured A. P. Hill. "I wonder if we can sue her."

"There's one other concern," said Bill. He explained about the simple real estate transaction, the power of attorney, and the Cayman Islands wire transfer while his partner's expression changed from polite bewilderment to apprehension and finally to utter dismay. "And so," Bill concluded, "I have hopes that Elizabeth will find the Confederate daughters and save me from being charged with fraud and murder."

"I see," said A. P. Hill. She was several shades paler now. Her eyebrows seemed to have arched permanently in an expression of horror.

"They were really very kind," Bill said.

"Except that they left you under suspicion of fraud and murder," his partner pointed out.

"The million and a half worries me," said Bill. "Will the state expect *me* to pay it back?"

"I hope not. We didn't get insurance on the practice yet, did we?"

"No. We opted for filing cabinets instead. I could never hope to raise that much money, Powell. I have the seventy-five thousand dollars from the house sale commission, but that wouldn't go far. Besides, I paid off my college loan with it and bought a car and the fax machine."

A. P. Hill groaned. "You shouldn't be let out alone," she said. "You have to pay taxes on that, remember! Are those all the assets you have?"

"All my worldly goods," said Bill. "Except for this." He fished out his Confederate penny and held it up with a rueful smile.

"Let me see that," said Powell, snatching the coin. "Where did you get this?"

"Miss Bridgeford gave it to me. For a lucky piece. You see. I told you those ladies were nice."

"They were very kind. Look, can I hold on to this for a little while?"

"Don't you think I need a lucky piece more than you do?" asked Bill.

"I promise to let you have the luck, partner. Right now I'd better go and talk to somebody about this little predicament of yours. We need to do something before you get indicted. I have our reputation to think of."

"Who can you talk to?" asked Bill. "I was afraid to go to any of the old boys in town, because if they find out how badly I've screwed up, we'll never get accepted by the legal eagles around here."

"I don't care for the thought myself," said Powell Hill. "But I can't see any way out of it. I'm going to see what I can do to clear up this mess. And then I suppose I'll have to talk to Cousin Stinky."

"Great!" groaned Bill. "Your cousin Stinky. You think a country lawyer from southwest Virginia can help me out? Where does Stinky practice? Martinsville?"

"Richmond. Cousin Stinky is the state's attorney general." A. P. Hill tossed the coin in the air and caught it. "Catch you later, partner."

"Let us cross over the river,
and rest in the shade of the trees."
—LAST WORDS OF STONEWALL JACKSON

CHAPTER

IO

''*Let me tell her* about it, Flora!" Lydia Bridgeford was saying. "After all, *I* discovered it!"

"But who put it there?" Dolly Hawks Smith demanded.

I was almost oblivious to their bickering, because the words *Confederate treasury* were still reverberating through my brain, louder than the cannons at Petersburg. "The Confederate treasury," I said, for perhaps the fifth time. "Wasn't it recovered by the U.S. Army at the close of the war?"

"Some of it," said Lydia Bridgeford. "One of the cabinet officers, a Mr. Micajah Clark, managed to account for about thirty thousand dollars, which he did turn over to the Union authorities. But remember that when Richmond fell, the government took the treasury with them to Danville. Gold bars."

I shook my head. "There couldn't have been much money. The Confederacy was poor. Our soldiers had no shoes, no ammunition, no meat—"

"I thought of that, too," said Flora Dabney. "But the Union blockade cut off the Confederacy's trade with other countries, which meant that there were no supplies to be had. That's not the same as being without the money to buy them."

"I have been tracing the Confederate treasury for some time now," said Lydia Bridgeford. "My dear father was one of the men responsible for guarding it."

"Your father stole the Confederate treasury?" I should have thought before I spoke, but, frankly, I was amazed to find that genteel larceny was hereditary.

Lydia Bridgeford was thoroughly indignant at such an improper suggestion. "Stole it from whom?" she demanded. "The government had fallen and the officials were trying to flee to Mexico. I am sure that he was keeping it in trust for a time when the South would rise again."

"Oh, Lyddy, he was not," said Dolly Smith. "You know perfectly well that your father spent his share and lost what he didn't spend in the crash of '29. What's buried here is *my* father's share." Her eyes twinkled as she revealed these ancestral misdemeanors. "Our fathers were young sailors assigned to guard the treasury," she explained. "And at some point after the retreat to Georgia, they took some of the gold bars entrusted to them and left for home. Lydia's father managed to sell his gold and became a prosperous legislator. My father buried his on this island."

"And you're only now coming back for it?" I was thinking that I wouldn't have waited until I was seventy to go in search of the family inheritance.

"I only learned of it recently," said Dolly Hawks Smith. "When we were going through our belongings as we packed to leave, Lydia found

an old letter from my father to her father. Father wrote it in 1901, long
before I was born, when his first wife died, and he thought his life was
coming to a close. I suppose he wanted his old friend to have the
money."

"Father hid the letter in a loose cover of the family Bible," said
Lydia. "I confess that I don't turn to it as often as I should, but really I
do think it was Providence that led me to find that letter as I was leafing
through it last month."

I looked at their beaming faces and at the metal detector resting
against the seat of the picnic table. "But how do you know that the gold
is still here?" I asked. "Mr. Bridgeford might have come back and dug
it up after he got the letter."

"I think he planned to," said Lydia. "After he lost all his money in
'29, he told Mother that we were going to a Georgia island to vacation.
I was only a little girl then, but I remember Mother remarking on how
strange it was that he'd want the expense of a seaside holiday when we
were in such dire financial straits. Anyway, we never came here. Father
had his stroke shortly after that. He was an invalid until he died."

"It's still here," said Flora Dabney. "And we intend to find it."

"Good," I said. "Then you won't be needing the million or so from
the sale of the house, will you?"

They gazed at each other with somber expressions. Finally Mary Lee
Pendleton said, "We don't want your brother to go to prison. If we find
the gold, we'll return the house money."

"In that case," I said, "I would be happy to work this metal detector
for you. An old boyfriend taught me how."

◆　◆　◆

If Cousin Stinky was glad to see the Hill family's newest
attorney, he concealed the emotion with remarkable skill. It might have
had something to do with the fact that "little Amy" had appeared at his
office without an appointment and with no apparent regard for his
schedule and prior commitments. It might have been the grim look of
determination she wore in lieu of the deferential simper he preferred
on a young female face. But most likely, it was the fact that with news-
men thick on the ground in Richmond government buildings, little Amy
Powell Hill had the audacity to come to his office in the middle of the

day wearing a Confederate officer's uniform, complete with sword and plumed hat. Stinky (who had scotched that nickname two hundred miles west of Richmond) barricaded himself behind his mahogany desk, and prepared to humor his eccentric young cousin for at least seven minutes—out of duty to the family.

"Well, Amy," he said genially, "have you embarked on a movie career? Is there a Civil War epic being produced in the vicinity?"

Powell Hill winced at the use of her first name, but she let it pass, saving her ammunition for bigger skirmishes. "No, sir," she replied. "I'm still practicing law."

"So I heard. I believe your mother said you had a tiny little practice in Danville. A low-rent affair. Have you tired of being stubborn already?" He rifled the papers on his desk, as if to indicate all the job openings he might be able to find for qualified young attorneys.

"No, I'm not tired of the practice," said A.P. "I'll stick it out, thanks. I came here to discuss two matters. One is my law partner, Bill Mac-Pherson. Your state legal beagles are hassling him because he accidentally sold the Home for Confederate Women."

"I've heard about that," said Stinky with an ill-concealed grin. "Is that young fellow your law partner? Oh, my. There's more than a million dollars unaccounted for, isn't there? And isn't he under some suspicion of having done away with the residents of the home?"

"I can clear that up." A. P. Hill reached into her briefcase and pulled out a fax message. "Here is a copy of an affidavit signed by all of the former residents of the home, indicating that they are alive and well and they removed the paperwork regarding the lien from the courthouse before my partner did the title search. And here's an agreement signed by John Huff, the present owner of the house, agreeing to sell the property back to the state for his purchase price plus ten percent." She paused and looked thoughtful. "I hope the restoration people were planning to do some remodeling. Mr. Huff seems to have done a lot of damage to the house. Holes dug in the yard, plaster removed from the walls . . . I take it he didn't find what he was looking for."

"Can we sue him?" asked the attorney general, momentarily distracted from the case at hand.

"You don't own the house, remember? I talked to a couple of my law professors about this. They agree with me that if no lien was present in the courthouse records, then the transaction was legal as it stood. Mr.

Huff bought the house fair and square. Bill was within his rights as an attorney to handle the sale. He is not liable for the money. Which"— she tapped the fax document from Jekyll Island—"the former residents admit to having in a numbered account in the Cayman Islands. They will not be returning to testify, by the way."

"This won't look good for your lawyer friend when it hits the papers, Amy."

"It won't hit the papers. That's where you come in. I want you to use all your influence to make this whole problem go away, because if you don't—"

Cousin Stinky frowned. The seven minutes were surely up by now. Why didn't his secretary buzz him? "If I don't—what?"

A. P. Hill stood up and straightened her plumed hat. "Why, Cousin Stinky, if we have any trouble at all about this matter, my entire regiment of Confederate reenactors will come and camp on the lawn of this building, and we'll give press conferences left and right telling people how the Commonwealth of Virginia evicted a bunch of senior citizens from their home because you were too cheap to pay their utilities! And I'll make sure the reporters know that *I'm* related to *you*."

"You wouldn't!"

"Sure I would," grinned Powell. "And I'd be sure to mention how the old ladies outsmarted you by stealing the documents, so that you'll have to spend nearly two million dollars of the taxpayers' money to buy the house back."

The attorney general's face had gone from good-old-boy red to the delicate green of aged cheese. The buzzer on his intercom sounded insistently, but he made no move to communicate with the caller. Finally he said, "I suppose I could speak to a few people and see that this gets hushed up." He had been considering running for a Senate seat in the next few months. A Confederate rally on his behalf would do nothing to help his chances at higher office.

"Good," said A. P. Hill. "I'll tell the boys to reschedule the rally for the other location."

"Reschedule it? But you said—"

"Oh, I'll leave you out of it," his cousin promised. "No one will know we're kin. But I'm going to stage a photogenic demonstration at the headquarters of the Park Service. That will give them one chance to back down before I sue them."

"You're suing the Park Service?"

A. P. Hill narrowed her eyes and set her jaw. "Damned straight. They told me that I couldn't participate in reenactments because I was a woman."

"So you're going to give them a real war instead, eh, Amy?" He was smiling in spite of himself, possibly at the thought of the legal fees that such a battle would generate.

"Yes. I'll fight them all the way to the Supreme Court if I have to. And I hope I have to."

The attorney general shook his head. "Legal battles like that can be both time-consuming and costly. I think you'd better drop this idea and get back to that struggling little practice of yours before you and your partner go broke."

"That brings me to the other thing I wanted to ask you about," said A. P. Hill. She reached into the pocket of her trousers and fished out a copper coin. "Do you know what this is? A Confederate penny piece. I had it verified at a coin shop before I came over here. Do you know how many there are in existence?"

"Can't say I do."

"Eight. They were made in Philadelphia as samples for the new government, but metal became scarce in the Confederacy, so pennies were never minted. This one must have belonged to one of the members of Jefferson Davis's cabinet. It's worth over half a million dollars."

"Where did you get it?"

"One of the Confederate ladies gave it to Bill. Her father acquired it after the fall of Richmond."

"Shouldn't you give it back, Amy?"

She shrugged. "Elizabeth MacPherson—that's Bill's sister—says that the women are leaving the country and they won't tell anybody where they're going. I guess they just don't trust your government, Stinky. Speaking of the government, I thought I'd ask you if the Commonwealth of Virginia would like to make us an offer for the coin before I put it up for auction. It would be a wonderful addition to the museum."

"I will consult with the appropriate officials," said her cousin cautiously.

"Great! Well, I guess that's it, then. Bill is off the hook—and I'm going to take on the Park Service." She patted her cousin on the shoulder. "Take it easy, Stink!"

The attorney general winced. "Goodbye, Amy. And could you please exit by the back way in case any reporters are lurking in the hall?"

◆　◆　◆

I-95 AGAIN. This time northbound. It's even more boring this time because it's a rerun of the previous days' drive. Same old pine trees, same old sandy soil. End of adventure. I felt a certain sense of accomplishment. The Confederate Eight, as I'd come to think of them, had been kind enough to draw up a notarized document attesting to their well-being and taking the blame for the real estate scam. I'd even bought a disposable camera at the drug store and taken a snapshot of them standing by the post office sign that said JEKYLL ISLAND. One of them was holding up today's newspaper, just in case anyone should doubt their affidavit. By now they would be packing to leave the Comfort Inn, heading for points unknown. I didn't ask. They weren't exactly the trusting type.

I will always remember them tramping through the sand in their crepe floral dresses, bickering about the directions in Gabriel Hawks's letter. Was *that* the oak tree that he meant? Exactly how long is a *pace*? And we kept getting interrupted by cars full of sightseers or people wanting to ask silly questions—like when was the island settled. As if we'd been there that long! By one in the afternoon it was becoming oppressively hot. Even the sea breeze had little effect. They wouldn't quit, though. Dolly Hawks Smith said that she for one wasn't getting any younger, and she didn't want to postpone the hunt for one more minute. The others agreed. I think, too, that they were afraid that since I had found them, other people might, too, and they were in a hurry to get moving again. We tried everybody's interpretation of which tree it was and how long a pace should be and when to turn left. But we always reached the same conclusion: that is, we ran out of island before we ran out of instructions.

"I don't understand," said Flora Dabney, swabbing her damp forehead with a little square of cambric. "Surely one of our interpretations might be right."

"And you're getting no reading on the metal detector?" asked Ellen Morrison with a worried frown.

"None," I said.

"Well, I can't figure out what we are doing wrong," said Lydia Bridgeford. "Of course, *my* father didn't write those instructions!"

"No," Dolly Smith replied. "Your father spent his gold as fast as he could."

"Wait," I said before the bickering could begin again. "There is a possibility we haven't considered. The directions could be perfectly correct—for 1865. But the island may have changed since then."

They looked at me with widening eyes, considering the implications of what I said. Finally Mary Lee Pendleton nodded and whispered, "Hurricanes."

"Yes. There have been quite a few bad hurricanes in the last hundred and thirty years, and at least half a dozen of them have hit this part of the eastern seaboard."

Ellen Morrison shivered. "I remember Hazel in '54. I was so frightened. I just stood at my window watching trees fall."

"So you think a storm has altered the island since Dolly's father buried his share of the gold here." It wasn't a question. Flora Dabney's tone said that she knew I was right.

"Look at the instructions," I said. "Go from that tree—or any of these trees for that matter—and walk twenty-five paces and turn left. You can't. And there are even more paces to walk after that, heading west. Do you see where that would put you?"

Dolly Hawks blinked back tears. "In the sea," she whispered.

"People get treasure out of the sea," said Lydia Bridgeford, patting her arm. "*National Geographic* had an article about some skin divers who found a sunken Spanish galleon."

"But it took them years," I reminded her. "And it cost millions. I don't think a saddlebag full of gold bars would be worth quite that much, even at today's gold prices. Maybe two million, tops. If you financed an expensive recovery operation, you'd be lucky to break even. And the publicity would alert the government, who would probably confiscate the gold anyhow. The Confederacy took it from the U.S. mint in the first place, remember?"

"Besides," said Ellen, "we probably wouldn't live to see the recovery anyhow. I say we take what we have and enjoy ourselves."

Flora Dabney gazed out at the sea with a thoughtful frown. "I had hoped we would have more than a million and a half. After all, there are eight of us. We'll have medical expenses."

"We can invest the money," said Mary Lee Pendleton. "If we don't live extravagantly, we'll be fine."

"We could always sign a book deal," said Dolly Smith. "I hear that pays well."

We went back to the inn after that and had seafood salads for lunch while we talked about what our respective ancestors did in the war. "But we mustn't go on about it too much," Flora Dabney whispered to me after my story about the Battle of Fort Fisher. "You know, poor dear Julia is the only soldier's *widow* here, but she isn't, strictly speaking, a Confederate woman. The late Mr. Hotchkiss was a Yankee from Abingdon. The mountains had a lot of Union sympathizers, you know."

"Why did you let her in the Home?" I whispered back.

"Well, dear, that was a long time ago. And we felt we had a great deal in common. It's our little secret."

Julia Hotchkiss reached for the last three hush puppies, blissfully unconcerned with her guilty secret.

After lunch, I left them to pack for points unknown and drove back to Danville—with nothing to think about but the other civil war in my life. MacPherson vs. MacPherson in divorce proceedings. *A house divided against itself cannot stand.* I wondered if I would prove any better than Abe Lincoln at preventing a secession.

◆ ◆ ◆

"Well, here we all are," I said brightly for the tenth time. I was smiling like a neon sign. I could feel every muscle in my face. "Here we are." I glared at Bill, mentally nudging him to say something positive, because I could feel my words falling with a crash into the center of this silent, strained family reunion. Our parents were in Bill's apartment, summoned at our request, politely sipping tepid white wine out of jelly glasses and behaving like hostages who were determined to be civil to their demented captors.

"Yep!" Bill caught my glare and straightened up with a nervous start. "Here we are," he chirped, flashing our parents an oafish grin, which they returned with plaster smiles.

They wouldn't look at each other. They sat as far apart as it is possible to get in the hamster cage that Bill calls a living room. Mother passed the time between sips by asking me carefully neutral questions about Cameron, and how things were in Scotland. She seemed determined to consider Dad a large, quaint piece of sculpture that she refused to comment on. Dad resembled a guilty schoolboy who has been hauled to the principal's office for a well-deserved whipping: determined to brazen it out by feigning indifference. Meanwhile my brother the host, to whom housecleaning is an unconfirmed rumor, kept offering to *run out to the store* for everything from napkins to crushed ice, but I knew better than to let him act on these alleged impulses of hospitality. He would run out to the store, all right. Probably to one in the next state, and he would contrive to prolong the errand until he could be sure his guests had fled. I wasn't about to be left holding this unsavory bag.

So there we were, all of us absolutely miserable, but determined to do a wooden impersonation of a normal family. In my fifth-grade history class we read the story about the little Spartan boy who put a fox cub in his tunic on the way to school, and then sat quietly through his lessons while the captive beast gnawed at his belly until the boy keeled over dead. That lad's spiritual descendants are my immediate family—and almost the entire population of my adopted country—and I am as exasperated about it as the fox was!

It was evident that my Waspish middle-class family members considered themselves far too well-bred to indulge in shouting matches or other forms of honest, but unseemly behavior. If left to their own devices, they were perfectly capable of making innocuous small talk for the entire interminable evening, while the real issues seethed below the surface, unexpressed, but tormenting everyone. Now, my life among the stiff-upper-lip crowd in Britain had not exactly enhanced my ability to advocate plain-speaking, but the knowledge that my stay in the United States was limited compelled me to introduce a little reality into the proceedings. I couldn't afford to wait out the months that would elapse between innuendo, ironic aside, inter-family conferences, and finally the reproachful understatement of a by-then-insoluble problem. I had a plane to catch.

In a lull just after Dad's monologue about the Cincinnati Reds and Mother's last question about the weather in Edinburgh, I said, "Look, folks, this is a charming family reunion, and I really appreciate your coming over to welcome me back, but could we stop shoveling the—the social pleasantries here and talk about what's really going on?"

Just for a fraction of a second they glanced at each other. Then after one of those little pauses, reminiscent of the silence between the lighting of the fuse and the instant of detonation, Mother said, "What is that, dear?"

"You told her about the separation yourself, remember?" said Bill. "And I told her everything else. Even the goldfish injunction."

Mother looked thoughtful. Finally she gave a little shrug, smiled, and said, "We have always tried to shield you children from any unpleasantness. I suppose, though, that you are no longer children."

"I was your attorney," Bill reminded her.

"Look," I said, hoping to forestall any embarrassing speeches about people drifting apart or the male mid-life crisis. "I'm sure that if you two find a qualified marriage counselor, you can work out whatever little problems are causing all this fuss."

"Problems?" said Daddy in that gruff voice he uses when he's annoyed. "We don't have any problems. We have simply decided to go on with our lives. You children are grown, so you are no longer a consideration in our staying together. So we decided to please ourselves."

"You certainly did," said Mother, with more than a touch of sarcasm.

"I'm seeing someone," Daddy muttered.

I think I said "Oh." I must have—because my mouth was in exactly that round shape that it forms when you say *oh*, except that I forgot to close it for quite some time afterward. I must have been mentally flipping through *Redbook* articles, trying to come up with an appropriate response. Finally I stammered, "Well, of course. You're at the dangerous age, aren't you, Daddy? Fear of mortality and all that. I'm sure the counselor will cover all that. I mean, you couldn't be seriously considering leaving Mother—"

Nobody said anything.

"And if marriage counseling is expensive, then I'd be happy to pay for the sessions," I said gently. "I can't stand by and see Mother's heart broken."

My mother chuckled.

Bill and I looked at her suspiciously. "Don't worry about me, you two. I don't want him back," she said.

"What?" we cried.

"Oh, for years I've been thinking that once you children were launched safely into the world, I'd be free to do what *I* want to do. Until now I've spent all my life being told what to do by some man. First there was Dad. Then I married Doug when I was too young to know who I wanted to be. Since then I've been a den mother, a bridge partner, a housekeeper, a wardrobe consultant, a chauffeur—but *I* got lost in the shuffle. Now I want to be Margaret, not Doug's wife or Bill and Elizabeth's mother. I suppose I wouldn't have had the courage to try life on my own, but when Doug had his hormone attack with that sweet young thing"—she giggled—"I decided that I was entitled to start over, too."

"She's just saying that," said Bill. "She doesn't want any of us to worry."

"I don't mind if you worry," Mother replied. "I certainly worried enough about you two when you were growing up. Since you seem to be concerned, I'll tell you that I'm going white-water rafting on the New River next weekend with Troy Anderson. I met him in my karate class at the community college."

"Karate class," Bill echoed.

"We'll be all right, kids," said Daddy, looking disgustingly cheerful. "But if you two need any counseling sessions to get over the trauma of your parents' divorce, I'll be happy to foot the bill."

Sarcasm is a very irritating habit. Unfortunately it runs in our family. It practically gallops. There seemed nothing left for me to do but return to Scotland, where my wonderfully unsarcastic husband was waiting.

My parents left after that. Daddy said he had dinner plans; Mother murmured something about expecting a phone call. Bill and I looked at each other across the table of half-full wine cups and shrugged.

"Well, we tried," said Bill. "And Mom is right. We are grown. Powell Hill tells me that the state has dropped the investigation. The law firm is solvent. I guess I'll be all right. And you have a husband and an inheritance, so you should be fine."

"Fine?" I echoed. Honestly, men have no sense of values. "Where are we supposed to have *Thanksgiving* now? And who gets the Christmas tree ornaments? And what about the tin punch picture I made for them at camp? Don't they care which one of them gets to keep that? Our whole history is being fragmented by a legal process."

"Yeah. Kind of makes you feel like an Eastern European country, doesn't it?" Bill mused.

"So you are going to let them do this?" I demanded.

He shrugged. "Mother fired me, remember? I don't think either of us can stop it. All we can do is try to stay close to both of them in their separate lives. And remember we've always got each other."

He beamed at me like an earnest sheepdog, and I patted his hand. "I'm so glad you're my brother, Bill," I said. "And not my attorney."